MURDER AT THE EMPRESS HOTEL

A Jillian Bradley
Mystery

Book 10

NANCY JILL THAMES

Murder at the Empress Hotel

Cover Design by LLewellen Designs:
www.lyndseylewellen.wordpress.com

Formatting by Libris in CAPS:
www.librisincaps.wordpress.com

Cover Photo Credits:
Female doctor/Zdenka Darula/Dreamstime.com
Beautiful Mature Woman/Rido/Dreamstime.com
Rose garden arches and patio/Dreamstime.com
Empress hotel at Night/Dreamstime.com
Yorkie 80220413/Shutterstock

Author Photo: Glamour Shots Barton Creek
Yorkshire terrier: *"Romeo"* Courtesy: Dan and Sara Olla
ISBN-10:1500671363
ISBN-13:978-1500671365
Category: *Fiction/Women Sleuths/Mystery & Detective/*

ACKNOWLEGEMENTS

This book could not have been written without the help of my husband Ted. Sincere appreciation also goes to Brenda Burke Johnson who guided the writing one chapter at a time, and the fabulous Beta Team of Deborah Fox Belisario; Kathleen Chipps; Roxanne Day; Kelly Gorman; and Donna Montgomery. To God be the glory.

DEDICATION

To the First Nations of Vancouver Island

PROLOGUE

It was time to get away. Perhaps melancholy had set in due to not much excitement in my life beyond answering questions for my garden column.

The only bright spot in my life was the little family living in the large Victorian I'd once occupied.

After the tragic loss of my second husband, a change in my life was needed to help forget the past.

I had reasoned Walter and Cecilia needed more room now that my godson D.J. had been born.

The perfect solution had been to give them the house, renovate the old worker's cottage for myself, and live on the back of my property.

The young couple had been my friends ever since that first homicide case in Half Moon Bay years ago. Since I had no children, they had become my family.

I considered my yard again. Granted, flowers and shrubs were interesting, I suppose, but living in the Bay Area the weather rarely varied and could even be described as boring.

Unlike other parts of the country with heavy snow and freezing temperatures, in Clover Hills, there were always gardening tasks.

That's okay for the younger generation, but as a senior working on a computer several hours a day, my back rebelled.

I was actually ready to hire a gardener for the first time

in my life!

This caused a guilt trip to begin to sprout until I yanked it out of my emotional garden and settled for practicality.

With my new yard team in place coming every other week to mow and trim, I could finally relax and travel.

First on my bucket list was The Butchart Gardens near Victoria on Vancouver Island. This magic spot had been calling to me ever since I watched a fascinating documentary on their creation from an old quarry. Besides, I read they served lovely lunches and afternoon tea, my particular favorites.

Hmm. I also had readers in British Columbia, as I recalled, so it might be worth a visit to help connect and boost readership.

It would also be a perfect way to justify the cost of the trip. What's not to like?

A call one afternoon with an invitation from dear friends in Arizona that I'd helped in another homicide case cinched my plans.

Before long, I was packed and ready to go with my beloved companion, Teddy, a four and a half pound Yorkshire terrier with a nose for adventure.

CHAPTER ONE

My little Yorkie shivered as I held him close. Teddy had never been on the open water before. A few gentle strokes calmed him as our Black Ball ferry continued from Port Angeles to our destination, beautiful Vancouver Island.

This brave dog could survive the uncertainty. He'd been in far more stressful situations, notably the time we were separated in London a few years ago.

The memory made me shudder. A few wrinkles were added to my face that day. It didn't matter. As long as I maintained my ideal weight on my small frame, and friends continued to comment on not looking my 67 old years, I was content.

When Teddy looked at me with those concerned brown eyes, I kissed him on top of his head. He was so adorable I simply could not resist.

He whimpered as we passed both peninsulas surrounding either side of the harbor.

"Don't worry, my love," I said. "We're almost to the harbor. You'll enjoy all kinds of new things to smell, I promise."

When he heard the word "smell" Teddy's shivers subsided. He perked up his soft pointy ears and panted.

"No one can ever convince me this intelligent little creature doesn't understand English," I said to my friends who stood against the railing.

Dr. Arthur Wingate, an old botanist colleague, vegan to

the core, and his tan, trim wife Diana each gave Teddy a pat.

A recent concierge for a five star Phoenix hotel, Diana had taken a position as a hotel reviewer for one of the news sites which carried my "Ask Jillian" column.

"How are you enjoying retirement, Diana?" I asked.

"It's been great. This trip worked out as a perfect thank you gift for your help in getting me this new job."

Arthur put his arms around his wife and gave her a hug. "She wrangled an excellent package for the three of us at the Empress including a senior discount for their famed afternoon tea."

"We knew you'd enjoy it." Diana said. "It's a legendary experience."

"So I've heard. So are the Butchart Gardens. I can't wait to see them."

"Look." Arthur pointed to the view of distant mountains.

Sunlight broke through the clouds and glinted on the water as we entered Victoria's Outer Harbor.

Hydroplanes took off as others gracefully landed, reminding me of white birds skimming the water for fish. Tugboats and other sailing vessels loaded with what appeared to be tourists navigated the picturesque port.

A warm breeze brushed by and ruffled my long blonde hair. After I inhaled the pleasant air, I exhaled and turned to my friends. "It feels as if we've been transported."

"To the Mediterranean?" Arthur must have read my thoughts. "The weather here is temperate year round."

"No wonder the island's a favorite for retirees. I read all about the demographics before we came."

Arthur breathed in the sea air. "I read the same thing, except love birds like it, too. I've heard Victoria's is a town of the newly-wed and the nearly dead."

Diana glared at him.

"That's awful, darling," she chided. "Anyway, Victoria's supposed to be rather quaint, too."

"Quaint as in shopping, you mean?"

He rolled his eyes, and it made me chuckle.

"You do love to shop, don't you, Diana," I said remembering some of the beautiful outfits I'd seen her wear.

She grinned and quickly nodded, which made me chuckle out loud.

"I must say I got the better part of the bargain, Diana. A few years ago I invited you to visit the Bay Area, and I wound up as your guest to Victoria."

Diana hugged me. "Jillian, we can never repay you enough. If it wasn't for your help, Arthur might be in prison for murder. And, you did help me to get this dream job."

"It was my pleasure. Now listen, you two, I love exploring on my own. Don't feel you have to baby-sit me while we're here. If you do, I may not join you the next time."

We had a good laugh.

The ferry glided into port, passing motor boats and sailing vessels on either side.

"We're now in Victoria's Inner Harbor." Arthur nodded to the grand array of architecture, including the Parliament Buildings and the Empress Hotel.

"Impressive." I studied the different vessels moored along the docks, captivated by the big stationary ones. A few had slips next to them where smaller boats were anchored.

"I never thought there would be houseboats. Maybe I didn't look close enough in the photos on TripAdvisor®."

The small cottage I lived in came to mind. The truth was, at times, it becomes confining.

What would life be like to live on a boat where you can sail away whenever the desire hit?

Diana tapped my shoulder. "You have a faraway look. Is anything wrong?"

A loaded question.

"No. A daydream about life on one of those houseboats is all. Sometimes wanderlust creeps in."

She nodded. "We heard about Vincent."

How could I fool my friends? Vincent was the man I'd recently been in love with. We'd met through Arthur during a collaboration in Scottsdale five years ago.

"Have you heard how he is?"

Arthur stroked Teddy. "Word has it he needs caregivers now. Jillian, don't feel guilty because you didn't rush to his side. It's not what he wanted."

"I've accepted his wish." I shook myself and hugged Teddy for comfort. "We've pulled to shore."

"We're here." Diana led the way to their car parked below deck. I admired her quick step and the smart way she always dressed.

Teddy perked up his ears as if he knew his little paws would soon be on dry land, then gave me an expectant look.

"Yes, let's get you into your tote for safety until we can set you down for a walk."

I shouldn't have said that word. Whenever I mentioned it, Teddy burst with excitement and wanted to run around in circles.

Arthur chuckled in his deep, rich voice I loved to hear. "Don't worry, Teddy. There'll be plenty of opportunities for w.a.l.k.s. when we get to the hotel."

Diana and I had to laugh when Arthur spelled out the word.

Upon arrival at our destination, a handsome and cheerful valet greeted us. "Welcome to the Fairmont Empress."

The hotel was a massive Chateau built of stone and

brick with steeply pitched copper roofs, domed polygon turrets, and ornate gables with dormer windows.

The valet gave Teddy a pat, piled our luggage onto a cart, and stepped aside as we approached the front desk.

Dramatic was the only way to describe the public rooms on the ground floor, with linking staircases to the palm court, ballroom, dining room, and library.

In the lobby, a stunning oriental carpet covered most of the black marble floor. And the harbor view was breathtaking.

Wood paneled walls, elegant window treatments, and fabulous art created wonderful ambiance for our stay.

A young couple waited in line behind us. The man, who could have been foreign judging by his slightly bronze skin and aquiline nose, wore a dark suit and chatted in quiet whispers while the young woman held onto his every word. Honeymooners, perhaps.

The clerk spoke to Arthur. "One of our staff will help your party to the Gold Check In desk. It appears you've been upgraded. Mrs. Bradley is a celebrity."

Arthur and Diana exchanged glances, and smiled.

Another of the hotel staff came over and introduced himself, shaking my hand effusively.

"I'm Harold Simms, the hotel manager. We hope you'll enjoy your stay, Mrs. Bradley. Maybe you'll get some inspiration for your garden column. 'Ask Jillian' is quite popular here in our Weekender."

"Thank you. You are most kind. I'll pass that on to my publisher. One thing I *will* write about are the gorgeous hanging baskets I see everywhere. Absolutely beautiful."

Teddy barked a tiny, "Woof."

"Oh, I'm sorry," the manager said to him. "We welcome you, too. What is his name?"

"Teddy."

"Well, welcome, Teddy."

The attention caused Teddy to pant, which I have come

to learn means he's happy or thirsty.

I nodded toward the winding wrought iron staircase leading to the next floor.

"The hotel is lovely. I look forward to your afternoon tea."

"Thank you." Mr. Simms motioned to a courtyard peering in from an entry close by.

"Don't miss our stained glass dome."

"I've seen photos. Palm Court, right?"

"You've done your homework, Ms. Bradley."

"Oh, please do call me Jillian."

He found a brochure and pointed to the tea times. "You must excuse me, Jillian, I'm being paged."

He nodded to another staff member to take over.

At that moment someone behind me tapped my shoulder.

I turned around and faced the young couple I'd noticed. The woman with dark hair pulled back in a neat pony tail wore a business outfit that hid her curvaceous figure.

"Excuse me," she said, "but are you the Jillian Bradley who writes the column?"

"I am. Are you a fellow gardener?"

"Kelly Morrison." She smiled and offered her hand in a firm business fashion. Then she turned to her young man. "This is David Blackwolf, the lawyer I work with."

His smile dripped charm.

"A pleasure, ma'am."

Without offering his hand he turned to her. "Check in for us. I think we're on the Gold floor, too. I need to meet with Leo."

"Sure. See you later."

We watched the young lawyer walk across the lobby until he was confronted by a man with a slight limp. The two men appeared to be of aboriginal descent with dark hair and bronzed skin. They could have been brothers.

After the man with the limp pointed an angry finger in

David Blackwolf's chest, the two men separated and disappeared down a hall.

The young woman seemed chagrined by the man's behavior. "Don't mind them. They've been at each other for years. Badger Knight is a lawyer for First Nations."

"And David Blackwolf represents the opposite side?"

Kelly nodded. "How observant."

Arthur and Diana followed the bellman with our luggage right as a text popped up on my phone:

Don't worry. Finish your conversation. We'll check in for you and let you know our room numbers.

I waved an acknowledgment.

"Is your fiancé aboriginal?" I asked. "His last name is Blackwolf."

The young woman blushed. She raised her hand to cover her mouth as if embarrassed. On her wrist jingled a pretty charm bracelet.

"So I guessed wrong," I said.

"No. David *is* a First Nations member, half-blood, actually, but he's only a good friend. We work together."

"I see. Sometimes good friends turn into more. But don't mind me. I'm a notorious matchmaker."

She smiled and another blush rose in her cheeks.

I pointed to her wrist. "Your bracelet is so unusual. The turquoise beads add a different touch."

"Thank you. David bought it for me one time when we were out together. He can be extremely kind. Or charismatic. He *is* a lawyer."

"Which would explain his demeanor. The lawyers I've known have all been the same way, in addition to being smart and clever. They seem to get what they want."

"Your dog is adorable!" She let him smell her hand, and scratched behind his ears. "My parents have a Yorkie. They love him to death. If I didn't work all day and live in a small apartment, I'd get one myself."

"Are you a lawyer, too?"

"I'm the administrative assistant to Leo Hunter. He's the department director for Fisheries and Oceans in Canada. David represents us."

"And do you have a meeting here at the Empress?"

"Yes. The conference rooms are connected through the conservatory." She checked her phone.

"I'd better check in and get back to work. David will wonder what's become of me."

"It's nice to meet a fan," I replied.

"Woof," Teddy barked.

"I'd better take him outside before I go to my room. Maybe we'll see each other later."

"I can't wait to tell Mom and Dad I met you." She took a card from her purse and handed it to me. "Let me know what room you're in so I can invite you to lunch while you're here."

"How nice." Kelly reminded me a little of my former personal assistant Cecilia back in Clover Hills. I took the card and tucked it inside with Teddy.

After Diana texted the room numbers, I sent a quick reply asking her to have the bellman settle my luggage.

I turned to my small companion.

"Let's go find a pet area."

Teddy wagged his tail at the idea.

CHAPTER TWO

Across the street from our hotel a sound of distant drums caught our attention. Teddy scratched the ground and dug up grass with his hind legs as an indication he was ready to leave and explore.

From hallmark totem poles rising behind some sort of Indian demonstration, I figured this was Thunderbird Park, a famed tourist destination outside the Royal British Columbia Museum of Natural History.

A small crowd gathered to watch a dance performed by a group dressed in traditional indigenous costumes. Or maybe this was their regular clothing. I didn't know much about their native culture.

Teddy watched one dancer in particular as she moved with graceful hands to the haunting music of drums and flutes.

The lovely Indian maiden, who looked to be in her early twenties, was dressed in a costume of cobalt blue adorned with bright beaded symbols. She wore her hair in braids wrapped in fur.

We moved in closer to hear an interpreter telling her story. The man was rather stout and appeared close to my age. He wore khaki Bermuda shorts, a First Nations tee shirt, and his grayish blond hair clutched in a small pony tail.

Next to him sat a man with arms crossed and a face of stone. I judged him to be in his late fifties. Unlike the interpreter, he dressed in contemporary clothing, wore glasses, and paid close attention to the performance.

Leaning against the wall behind him appeared to be a few tribal artifacts.

The dance was fascinating to watch.

Teddy must have thought so, too. He sat erect on the ground and didn't move a muscle.

After the demonstration ended it was followed by polite applause, including mine. I approached the interpreter and extended my hand.

"What a wonderful performance! I was transported."

"Thank you."

Teddy reached out a paw.

"It looks as if your dog wants to be introduced." He bent down and shook it. "I'm Father Goodman."

"Woof," Teddy barked.

The man's name sounded familiar. We shook hands.

"I'm Jillian Bradley, and this is Teddy."

"I recognize you from your column, Mrs. Bradley. You look exactly like your picture."

"*Father* Goodman?"

He chuckled in a jolly fashion, then reached down and picked up Teddy, who lavished him with dog kisses.

"Uh-huh. I get the same reaction every so often. Although I *am* a priest, I'm also a professor of continuing studies at Royal Roads University."

"I'm impressed. Oh, don't get me wrong. I get the informality in this setting. I simply wondered if you knew a dear friend of mine who has a parish in Canyon Grove, near my home. His name is Father Perkins."

"In California?"

I nodded.

"Tall? Lanky?"

"That's him."

The priest slapped his thigh. "We were in seminary together. Come to think of it, he sent me a note and told me you planned to visit. Said he saw you at a wedding or somewhere."

"Right. My niece Annika and her fiancé wed last month. Father Perkins performed the ceremony. I must have mentioned my trip."

The female dancer I had watched came toward us, followed by a familiar looking young man who walked with a limp. It was the same lawyer who had the confrontation with David Blackwolf!

"Ah, Rainbow." Father Goodman ushered the woman, now freeing her braids from fur, in my direction. "Meet Jillian Bradley, the famous garden columnist, and her dog, Teddy. Jillian Bradley, this is Rainbow Knight."

"A lovely name, Rainbow. Your dance was mesmerizing. Teddy enjoyed it, too. He stood still for the entire performance."

She smiled. "I'm flattered." Her voice resonated with an intelligence that matched her beauty.

In contrast to her gentle spirit, she introduced the disgruntled looking man beside her. "This is my brother, Badger Knight."

"Yes, Kelly Morrison told me who you were." I waited for his reaction. When he didn't respond, I let go the fact I'd seen him in a conversation with David Blackwolf at the Empress a few moments ago.

His angry look grew darker. "I'm sorry. I have a meeting. If you'll excuse me." Badger headed toward the hotel.

A voice from behind startled me.

"You must forgive Badger." It was the stone faced man who had focused on the dancers. "He has much on his mind which clouds his manners. I am Raymond Crow, elder spokesman for the First Nations."

"It's an honor to meet you."

As we shook hands, he radiated warmth.

Father Goodman handed Teddy to me.

"You said you are the spokesman?"

He bowed his head, then lifted his eyes. "I am an elder of the Songhees Nation and represent my people in matters which concern them."

Father Goodman leaned in. "The Canada Department of Fisheries and Oceans arranged a conference between their representatives and First Nations at the hotel. This pow wow was to encourage aboriginals to attend in support."

"I will see you at the meeting," the tribal leader said.

The priest nodded in respect as the elder left.

I looked around and studied the crowd. The majority of the audience appeared to be tourists by the way they had been videotaping the dancers.

"The performers and I need to get over there as soon as possible." He scanned the dispersing group.

"Rainbow, where is Gerald?"

She gathered her purse. "He said he needed to help set up your things."

"Gerald Dawson is my assistant professor. Rainbow is one of my grad students."

"I can see you're busy," I said. "I'll let you go. A pleasure to meet you."

"Oh, I'm sorry, Mrs. Bradley." Father Goodman seemed distracted. "You may want to sit in on the first session in about thirty minutes. It will give you a true perspective on how aboriginals are treated."

I thought of how the American Indians had been treated. It made me sad.

"Perhaps I will poke my head in. First, however, I need to touch base with my hosts. Thank you again for a wonderful demonstration, Rainbow."

She smiled. "Perhaps we'll see you at the session." Was this a plea?

"I'll do my best." I set Teddy on the ground. "Come along, boy. We'd better hurry."

"There you are!" Arthur ushered me into their room. "Did you figure out how to use the elevator to get to us?"

"Not at all."

Teddy panted from the walk.

"Lucky for me, the bellman offered to help when I explained my plight of not having my key to the Gold Floor. We used his to gain access."

"Teddy looks thirsty," Diana said.

"May I borrow a cup for some water?"

Arthur gestured to the mini bar. "Be our guest."

Diana handed me a key. "Here's yours. Your room's next door. Arthur and I checked out the Gold Lounge. You'll love it, Jillian."

"I'm sure I will."

I explained about the meeting I was asked to attend, and assured them I could easily use the excuse of having Teddy to think of.

Diana shook her head. "Nonsense. We'll be happy to watch him. Arthur and I were going to relax in the room anyway."

With Teddy situated with Arthur and Diana, I headed toward the conference center and found the room designated for First Nations and Department of Fisheries and Oceans.

A handful of observers were in the audience. I sat in back of the room in case I wanted to make an early departure.

Father Goodman approached. "I wonder if you'd consider sitting closer to the front. Not many of our constituents are here, and we need the support." He reached inside his pants pocket. "And before I forget, here's my card. Call me if you need anything while you're here in Victoria."

"Of course." So I wouldn't be able to leave early after all.

The young woman I'd met in line when I checked into the hotel waved. She spoke to a man sitting on the platform and nodded my way. He turned out to be the man Father Goodman was about to introduce.

Leo Hunter's formal introduction by the priest was met with a tepid response from the audience. Hunter reminded me of a lion with his strawberry blond mane and intense expression.

When Raymond Crow was introduced, the crowd showed clear favoritism.

Badger Knight held a somber look throughout the proceedings, while David Blackwolf gave off an air of decided confidence.

The rivalry was obvious. At one point a request by a commercial fishery to build on a tribal fishing ground was introduced by Kelly's lawyer friend. Badger met him with so much opposition, they almost came to blows. Badger's name fit his body language.

Another rather skinny young man, who wore dark, horned rimmed glasses, watched the two. His raised eyebrows suggested disbelief at the unfolding drama as he hovered around Father Goodman and Rainbow — mostly around Rainbow, I noted.

I assumed he must be Gerald Dawson, Father Goodman's assistant professor.

Father Goodman stood. "I believe we need a recess. We'll take a fifteen minute break."

David Blackwolf smiled as he met with Leo Hunter, the man the priest had introduced at the first of the meeting. Hunter now patted David on the back. The two looked confident.

"Jillian!" Kelly beamed as she approached. "I want to introduce you to Leo Hunter, the man I work for."

We walked over to where the two men stood talking.

"Excuse me, Leo. I want you to meet Jillian Bradley, the famous garden columnist."

"How do you do, Mrs. Bradley?" he said. "I didn't realize someone like you would be interested in fishing affairs."

The man sounded condescending.

"I'm always interested in the underdog, Mr. Hunter."

He raised an eyebrow and returned to his seat on the panel.

After the break, a discussion of unfair treatment over fishing rights ensued, most of which was in legal terms which were hard to follow.

I left with a conclusion that the Canadian government had not upheld their promises to protect fishing rights of the First Nations.

It seemed typical treatment of an indigenous society, run off their own land by an aggressor.

What was not typical, however, was that the opposing lawyers gave the impression they were descended from the same folk.

One argued for economic advancement, while the other defended the protection of centuries-old traditions.

I needed to be alone for a minute with a nice cup of tea. A visit to the Gold Lounge would be perfect. I sent a text to Diana, asking their indulgence.

The confrontation between the two young lawyers had left me uneasy.

So did Leo Hunter.

CHAPTER THREE

After finishing a nice cup of tea, the attendant removed my empty cup. "Enjoy the rest of your afternoon, Mrs. Bradley."

Did everyone know my name?

"Thank you." Feeling revived, I left the elegant sofa and headed to Arthur and Diana's room across the hall. After a few knocks, the door opened.

"There you are!" Arthur held tight as Teddy squirmed to get down. "You'd better take him before he tries to jump into your arms."

"Come here, little one." After a hug, I kissed him on top of his head. I turned to Arthur. "Thanks for dog-sitting."

Diana chuckled. "Arthur loved it. He and Teddy played fetch until the poor thing tuckered out."

"Arthur or Teddy?"

We all laughed.

"How did your meeting go?" Arthur asked politely.

"Let's say I'm glad it's over. Think white man verses American Indian and you'll understand."

"Oh, dear." Diana shook her head. "Repression goes on in Canada, too?"

I nodded.

Diana cocked her head. "You look tired. Are you up to going out again?"

"Why don't you two have a nice dinner together tonight?" I suggested. "I want to settle in and relax. If I get hungry, I'll go to the Gold Lounge for hors d'oeuvres."

"What about Teddy?" Diana asked.

"I'll carry him until I get my food and carry it back to the room. I brought Teddy's in his insulated lunch box."

"Jillian," Arthur said, "you're too much!"

I smiled. "Have fun, you two."

I attached Teddy's red rhinestone leash and led him to our room next door.

To my surprise, there was a fresh bouquet of flowers on the bathroom counter, a basket of fruit and snacks, and a bottle of wine on the chair ottoman.

A note read: Welcome to the Fairmont Empress, Mrs. Bradley. We hope you enjoy your stay. From our staff.

How lovely, I thought, before returning to the reality that I was caregiver to my dog.

After I put his food in the small fridge, I kicked off my shoes and walked to the window.

The harbor view sparkled with lights from boats and the magnificent Parliament Buildings now fully lit in the twilight. Victoria lived up to the name of Canada's most beautiful city.

I turned on a classical FM station, stretched out on the sofa with Teddy, and listened to Debussy's *Clair de Lune*. It soothed my soul, as it always does.

Thank you, Lord, for this wonderful and much needed getaway.

The respite didn't last long.

"Woof!" Teddy barked.

I checked the time. "You're hungry, aren't you? Me, too. Let's take a peek in the Gold Lounge and see what the dinner offerings are."

At the word "dinner," Teddy's ears shot up as if to say, "I'm ready whenever you are, Mistress."

Nestled in his new Cheetah carrier, the two of us entered the Gold Lounge with a few guests in line for appetizers. Smiles crossed most of their faces the moment they saw

Teddy. One or two seemed off-put or had no reaction.

It didn't matter to me.

I joined the line, took a plate, and selected a bacon wrapped scallop, a slice of cold salmon, a few shrimp and some cocktail sauce. For the two of us I added fruit, crackers, and raw veggies, with a few cubes of cheese for me.

It was supposed to be an unhealthy trend for dogs to eat cheese, although I'd fed it to my previous Yorkies for years without incident.

With a bottle of water stuffed along with Teddy, I was ready to carry the full plate back to our room where we enjoyed our splendid meal.

After we ate, I took Teddy for a brief walk along the harbor. A gentle sea breeze blew, and I took another deep breath. Fisherman's Wharf brimmed with interesting places to visit while we were here.

While tidying the room and putting Teddy's things away, the card Kelly had given me fell to the floor. I sent a brief text to give her the room number.

To my surprise, she sent an immediate text back with an invitation to lunch the following day.

I sent a reply:

Will check plans with my friends and let you know.

As is my habit, I laid out an outfit for the next day so I wouldn't have to think about what to wear when my mind was not fully awake.

"This black stripe shirt over a camisole will do nicely," I said to myself. "Now for a nice hot bubble bath with bath salts to soothe my tired feet."

After I had soaked enough, the time came to dry off, don my nightie, and spritz on perfume to insure pleasant dreams.

"Come along, sweet doggie. Time to turn off the lights." I picked him up, gave him a hug and settled him on a towel at the foot of my bed.

"Night, night." I said, glad of his company.

Everything was quiet except for a few voices which passed in the hall outside, nothing unusual for a hotel. The walls did seem a little thin, but it was an old hotel built in 1908.

We drifted off to sleep, until a noise from the next room woke me up. It wasn't from Arthur and Diana's because theirs was on the other side.

The clock showed 10:53 pm.

Teddy was on alert. He jumped off the bed and raced to the door.

"Woof, woof!" he barked over and over until I had to shush him.

I grabbed a hotel robe from the closet and threw it on.

Teddy scratched as fast as he could, wanting to leave. I sensed someone might be in trouble.

I let him out, then raced to grab him.

He stopped in front of the room next to mine and pawed the door.

I knocked. No answer.

Teddy whined.

All I could do was wake Arthur and ask for his help.

"Call 911 or get someone to open the room next to mine. Hurry!" I whispered. "Someone may be in trouble."

Arthur didn't hesitate. "Right, Jillian. I'll call the front desk."

Within minutes one of the staff unlocked my neighbor's door and went inside.

Teddy and I rushed in behind.

My hand flew to my mouth!

Behind an overturned easy chair on the floor stretched a pair of legs. Maybe this was what Teddy and I heard.

The body lay on its back with the head turned to one side, lifeless and still.

There was a swollen mark on the back of the neck where it appeared the man had been struck from behind. A strange looking weapon was lodged in his chest.

The stick was about three feet in length marked with images similar to the ones on the totems I had seen yesterday afternoon, which suggested it might be aboriginal.

"I'll check his pulse." The staffer bent down. When he looked up and shook his head, I knew the man was dead.

And then I recognized his face.

It was David Blackwolf!

"I'll call the police," the staffer said.

I grabbed Teddy, who'd been sniffing the carpet, and perused the suite, careful not to contaminate evidence. I'd been in situations like this before.

There was a bedroom with an unmade bed, but no sign of a struggle. On the counter of the wet bar sat two empty glasses and a bottle of some sort of spirits.

The glasses were clean, as if they had not been touched.

I noticed the window drapes were open. When I took a closer look, I could see the window wasn't locked.

The ominous stick which protruded out of his chest was definitely aboriginal. It reminded me of something I'd seen recently, but couldn't be sure what it was or where I'd seen it.

"Excuse me, ma'am," a voice said.

I turned to see several policemen. The heavyset one in front stepped toward me and Teddy.

"Officer, my dog sensed this man was in trouble. His name was David Blackwolf."

"I recognize him. I'm Sergeant Nick Stone. Would you please step away from the body?"

"Oh, of course. I'm so sorry. I'm Jillian Bradley, and this is Teddy."

"Woof!" Teddy barked.

I scooped him up and held him close.

Sergeant Stone ignored Teddy, drew tweezers from his pocket and stooped down to retrieve a small object.

"Men," Stone said, "Disperse the crowd. And get the tape up, now!"

The officers did as he said.

Arthur sent another text:

We'll wait for you in our room. Good luck!

Sergeant Stone gestured for me to take a seat, made a call, and studied the body for several minutes. He took a sack of candy from an inside pocket, reached in and got a handful of cinnamon candies, popping them in his mouth.

"Please tell me what happened, ma'am. From the beginning."

I told him everything, from the moment we arrived until he walked through the door. After I finished, he made another call.

"Get out an APB on Badger Knight and Kelly Morrison. And hurry."

My eyes widened. Had Badger murdered David over some dispute? Surely it went deeper. They were professionals!

"Mrs. Bradley, thank you for your cooperation. I know you're a celebrity and hope you appreciate the fact serious crimes are rare in Victoria. I hope you'll allow us to contact you if we need to speak to you further. Otherwise, you're free to go."

"Thank you, Sergeant, but I did notice a mark as if someone struck him on the back of his head and stabbed him afterward."

I was not allowed to finish what I had to say.

"Officer Ramsey," Sergeant Stone said, "please escort Mrs. Bradley back to her room."

"No need, officer. Teddy and I are ready to leave." I made my way into the hall, and motioned to Arthur's room. "I'm one door down if you need to talk to me."

"Goodnight, Mrs. Bradley."

Another officer finished the sealing tape, then closed the door.

I held Teddy close as we walked to Arthur and Diana's room. After I stepped inside, I cried.

Diana held me. "Did you know him?"

I nodded. "We'd been introduced. He was a good friend of the woman I chatted with in the lobby when you and Arthur left to finish our check in. I overheard Sergeant Stone put out an APB on her."

"So she'll know soon enough." Arthur gave Teddy a pat. "I'll walk you back to your room."

"Thanks. We'll talk in the morning, Diana. Goodnight."

I was still shaky as I slipped back beneath the covers.

Teddy curled beside me. His warmth calmed.

Where had I seen that stick before? I closed my eyes and tried to think.

But all I could see was a murder weapon.

I had to remember!

CHAPTER FOUR

The next morning my phone beeped with a text message. I struggled to open my eyes as I remembered a horrible dream. A man lay dead, struck down by a spear.

I sat up.

Teddy stretched on his towel, wagged his tail, and climbed onto my lap.

"Hello, love. Let's see who's sent a message."

It was from Diana:

Breakfast, Gold Lounge, 9:30 am.

I typed a happy face symbol :).

"Time to get dressed, take you out, and make you something to eat."

"Woof." Teddy agreed.

I donned an outfit of dressy jeans, a fancy top and short boots, got Teddy ready for his walk and stepped into the hall.

It hadn't been a dream.

Crime scene tape covered the opening of the room next to mine. The forensics team carried out a large container of evidence.

One of the men waved his arm. "Excuse us, ma'am. We need to pass."

I stepped aside.

Sergeant Stone closed the door. "Ah, Mrs. Bradley. Going somewhere?"

"For a short walk. Teddy needs to sniff the grass."

He cracked a smile.

"Any suspects yet? Did you find Kelly or Badger last night?"

"No to your first question. As for the second, we did locate those persons of interest."

I smiled my nicest smile. "Are you finished here? You're welcome to join us on the way down."

"Why not?"

I still had time before Arthur and Diana.

"Sergeant, did David and Badger come from the same tribe?"

"As a matter of fact, they did. According to the records anyway."

"I see. Does this mean you've taken Badger into custody?"

He eyed me. "What makes you so interested in this case? You don't have any connections, do you?"

"Connections?" I shrugged. "It's just my curious nature. I enjoy solving puzzles. If you ask certain folks, they may tell you I'm good at it."

"I see. Who, for instance?"

We'd reached the ground floor.

"Come with me outside and I'll tell you."

Stone looked as if he needed exercise. He was heavy set with a paunch, which covered his belt buckle.

Teddy led the way and almost pulled me along. He'd only been to the place once, but remembered how to get there.

"Do you take your dog everywhere?"

"Wherever I can. I'm a widow. It gets lonely."

"I'm married with five grown children. Wife's a stay-at-home grandma now. Used to be a stay-at-home mom, but now all the moms work."

"So your wife baby-sits."

He nodded. "House is always a mess, but we love the grandkids."

We reached an area for Teddy.

Teddy reveled in the grass, wagged his tail, and panted.

"Woof!" he barked.

Sergeant Stone panted, too.

We found a bench.

"Mrs. Bradley." He looked at the ground, and then at me.

"My friends call me Jillian."

"Jillian. You understand I can't discuss this case."

"Oh, absolutely! I would never breach protocol unless it helped find the murderer."

"I'm glad we have an understanding."

"You're only doing your job. I'm sure you'll have no trouble figuring out who the murderer is."

"I appreciate your cooperation, Jillian. You can give me a list of your references in case I have any theoretical questions."

I took my phone and using my microphone to save time, recorded him a list:

Chief Inspector Gordon Halsey, New Scotland Yard; Sheriff Mark Taylor, Lake Placid, NY; Chief Frank Viscuglia, Half Moon Bay, CA; Detective Robert McKenzie, San Diego, CA; Detective Jack Noble, Scottsdale, AZ and Detective Walter Montoya, Clover Hills, CA.

"Give me your email and I'll send it to you."

Sergeant Stones quirked an eyebrow as he listened.

"This is quite a list. I'd say you have some experience."

"And I'd say we caught the bad guys. Come along, Teddy. It's time for breakfast."

Sergeant Stone scratched his bald head.

Back in the room, I put out fresh water and made a meal for Teddy from some of the food I'd brought for him.

The Empress provided food and water dishes, along with their in-house barley baked dog treats. Teddy ate them, no problem.

Now it was my turn to think about lunch.

I took Teddy's things from the closet and remembered I hadn't replied to Kelly about getting together. A good excuse as any to talk with her, so I sent a text:

Are you free for lunch today? I heard what happened. I'm so sorry and will understand if it won't work out. Jillian

She replied at once:

I'd appreciate the company. Anywhere but the hotel. Fisherman's wharf would be okay. Meet you at Grilligan's at 12:30 pm. Kelly

I texted back:

See you at 12:30 pm. Jillian

Kelly must be devastated. I'd been there and understood the importance of support. She'd mentioned her parents, and sounded as if they were close.

Perhaps they lived on the mainland and found it too early to join her.

I always tried to understand people. In Kelly's case, from the way she talked about her parents, it sounded as if she was still dependent on them. Perhaps they were all she had.

I shook my thoughts back to the job at hand.

"Let's get you into your carrier, sweet pup. We're almost late for breakfast."

Teddy snuggled inside his carrier and went to sleep. Good dog.

Arthur and Diana waited at a table in the far corner.

I gave a nod, walked to where they were seated, and plunked Teddy on the floor.

"I'll be right back. Watch the baby for me, please."

Diana peeked at Teddy, sound asleep.

"It won't be a problem. What an angel!"

I left to fill my plate with scrambled eggs mixed with ham and cheese, fresh fruit, and a chocolate croissant. (How could I resist?)

An attendant approached after I rejoined Arthur and Diana.

He smiled. "Coffee, Mrs. Bradley?"

"Yes, thank you. Black is fine."

"Would you care for any juice?"

"Tomato, no ice, would be lovely, thanks."

He left and returned with a tall glass garnished with a slice of lemon.

"Great service, don't you think?" Arthur smiled at Diana.

"It's been impeccable, except for the murder." Diana shivered.

"Are you going to get involved, Jillian?" she asked.

"I may be already."

They exchanged looks.

"You think the police will let you?" Arthur looked skeptical.

I sipped the juice and sampled the eggs. "It may take some time, but I gave Sergeant Stone enough references to get my foot in the door."

Diana nodded at Teddy. "Did you tell him about Teddy's special abilities?"

I shook my head.

"That will come later, when Stone is ready. Teddy was first on the scene, as I recall."

He poked up his head hearing his name.

I wondered if he was listening. My sleuth dog, as I affectionately called him, loved praise, and praise for finding clues most of all.

"I hope you don't mind, but I'm having lunch with Kelly Morrison. She invited me when we met and would appreciate the company after what happened last night."

Arthur wiped his mouth and sipped his water.

"I'm stuffed." Diana leaned back. "That works for us. The hotel is giving us a personal tour for my review. Lunch is on them today."

Arthur stood, and helped Diana from her chair.

"Be careful, Jillian." She put her hand on my shoulder.

Arthur whispered. "Don't take any unnecessary chances."

"I won't. We're having lunch on the wharf, and Teddy will be with me. You two run along and enjoy your day."

Arthur peered into my empty cup.

"I'll have the server bring you a refill."

"You're too good to me." I smiled.

"Take care, Jillian." Diana hugged me.

Lord, thank you for good friends.

Please protect me.

CHAPTER FIVE

Since lunch was several blocks away, I decided to take advantage of the horse drawn carriage parked nearby. It was the first time I'd ever ridden in one, but it wouldn't be the last. Teddy loved smelling the air as the horses clopped along.

Kelly waited in front of Grilligan's, a colorful yellow, blue and green little bistro with an order window for kayakers still in their boats. Not something one sees every day.

After ordering turkey pita sandwiches and waters with lemon, we found a quiet place to sit overlooking the harbor.

Teddy sat alert at my feet, ready for any morsel of sandwich I cared to share.

"He's so cute," Kelly said. "How long have you had him?"

"Ever since my niece moved to an apartment. They didn't take pets."

We shared a chuckle, then bit into our pitas.

"How's everything going with your conference, now that there's been this unfortunate incident?" I asked in between bites.

Kelly shook her head.

"Awful. Things are in an uproar and the discussions are at a complete stop."

"Understandable."

She set her sandwich down and looked at me. "This is

like a dream – a surreal one. Leo gave me the day off until further notice. He's talking to the police this afternoon."

"I see. Have you had a chance to talk to them?"

She sat back. "I met with them and gave a statement. Jillian, David's room was right next to mine and I didn't hear a sound. Maybe if I had he'd still be alive."

"Don't feel bad. If it hadn't been for Teddy getting upset, I probably would've ignored the situation."

"Teddy got upset?"

"When he heard the noise it was if he turned into a homing pigeon. He barked and scratched at the door until I opened it and followed him."

"So did you find the body?"

I nodded. "We had a staff member open the room."

She paled.

"It wasn't the first body I'd seen. Still, it was horrible to see him lying there. I probably shouldn't talk about it. The police expect things to stay hush-hush."

"I understand. Sure hope they find out who killed him. Seems incredible to me."

"Kelly, did David have any enemies?"

She slowly shook her head as if trying to recall. "Badger Knight wasn't a friend exactly, but they were both from the Songhees Nation. They grew up together."

"I thought of him, too. Did Badger ever threaten David?"

"Oh sure, but it was only talk. At least that's the way it sounded whenever Badger got angry."

I remembered their confrontation at the hotel.

Kelly picked up the last of her sandwich and finished it.

"There must have been an underlying reason. Lawyers deal with issues all the time without getting emotional," I said.

She took a sip of water, then set the glass down. "Ask someone in their tribe. I do know David was fond of Badger, in spite of the way he was treated."

"I'll see what I can find out."

Teddy stretched out his front paws, then his back ones.

I gave him the last bite.

"Better get moving. He gets restless after a while."

"Mind if I walk with you?" she asked, patting her tummy. "I need the exercise and could do with the company. I still feel unnerved by what happened."

"Not at all. Teddy, are you ready for a walk?"

He perked up his ears and wagged his tail furiously.

Kelly smiled. "I guess we can take that as a 'yes.'"

We strolled along the wharf, peering at boats unloading their catches. Tourist shops dotted the boardwalk, enticing buyers.

Teddy sniffed fish in the air.

"David and I came here once. It was when we first met."

Tears welled up.

"I am sorry, Kelly. I know you were fond of him."

She nodded, then wiped the tears away with her hand.

"Life goes on, I guess," she said. "You know what I think I'll miss the most?"

"What?"

"The way he made me feel, as if I really mattered."

"Did you spend much time together?"

She shrugged. "We rappelled on occasion. Rock climbing was his favorite. He loved the challenge of finding the next foot hold."

"Are there places on the island for rappelling?"

Teddy perked up his ears as if he sensed something fun to do.

"David had his special places. I went with him a couple of times when he didn't get any better offers."

"You mustn't put yourself down, Kelly. David wouldn't have bought you a pretty charm bracelet if he didn't value you somehow."

She looked at her wrist. "I couldn't bring myself to wear it. Every time I see it I think of him."

"That's understandable."

We'd reached the hotel. "Are you still staying here?" I asked.

"Only until Leo and I wrap up the files. After we finish, I'm going back to my apartment."

"Have you told your parents about David?"

"Not yet. They'd worry about my safety if I told them he was murdered next door to my room."

"Where do they live? Sorry if I'm nosy, but I'm interested in everyone."

"No, that's okay. It's nice to have someone to talk to who's not work related. My parents live close to me. I go over there to eat once a week so they can know what I'm up to."

As we parted ways in the hall, Kelly gave Teddy a pat. "Thanks again for lunch, Jillian."

"My pleasure. Call me if you want to chat."

"I will." She walked slowly to her room, looking downcast.

Once inside the room, I removed Teddy's red rhinestone leash and refreshed his water dish.

He lapped thirstily.

I gently dried his muzzle, gave him a hug, and plopped him down on a comfy chair. He turned around several times until he was comfortable, then watched me.

"What?" I asked. "Dinner isn't for several hours."

He continued to look at me as if something bothered him.

"Too bad you can't tell me what you're thinking, sweet dog."

He sighed, put his head on his paws, and closed his eyes

for a nap.

It was curious.

An unexpected text from Sergeant Stone blinked on my iPhone:

We have a problem. Need to talk. Name a time and place.

Since I'd had lunch not long ago, I offered to meet him for a cup of tea.

His answer was instantaneous:

Pick you up in 30 minutes.

Teddy could take the rest of his nap in his tote.

Sergeant Stone waited in the lobby with a serious look on his line etched face.

"Afternoon, Mrs. Bradley. The car's right outside."

Thank heavens we didn't have to walk. I needed a nap after this.

"Sergeant." I nodded. "Please call me Jillian. Mrs. Bradley makes me feel ancient."

"Sorry, ma'am. Mrs. Bradley will do fine."

A stubborn man. Perhaps it was for the best to keep things professional.

Without a word, Stone got in the car, leaving us to climb in on our own.

Fine.

"We'll be having tea at Murchies. Nice and close." He nodded ahead.

A lit marquee overhead welcomed us to enter the huge coffee and tea shop. Never had I seen a wider selection.

The pastry case enticed, but I resisted.

Not Sergeant Stone.

He pointed to a decadent cream filled Napoleon. "I'll have that one."

"Nothing for me, thanks," I said. "Only tea, three sugars."

Stone gave me a look.

I didn't flinch.

"Tea for me too, please. Milk. No sugar."

It was quite early. He led the way to an out of the way table, set down his pastry and tea, and drew out what appeared to be a newspaper clipping.

With Teddy happily down for the rest of his nap on the floor, I took a seat.

"What do you have there?" I asked.

"Wife wanted your autograph. She's a huge fan. Swears you know everything about gardening."

I took the clipping, then reached into my purse for a pen. "What's her name?"

"Penelope."

"To Penelope, All my best. Jillian Bradley." I handed it back.

"Thanks. She'll appreciate it." He tucked the note back inside his pocket. "We've had an unforeseen development with the Blackwolf case."

"And you're willing to share with a layman?"

"Layman? Evidently that's not the case after checking those references."

"How can I help?"

"We thought this case would be open and shut. However, we didn't count on the security system upgrading at the time of the murder."

"I see. Bad luck." I sipped my tea and waited.

"Which means, aside from Blackwolf's business associates, we don't know where to start."

"Who have you talked to?"

"I took statements from Kelly Morrison and Leo Hunter. Badger Knight still hasn't surfaced, but we'll find him."

"Have you checked with his people?"

"First Nations?"

I nodded.

"It will have to be a special trip. We work with their law enforcement agency in these cases."

Teddy rolled over and resettled. I reached down and

patted him back to sleep.

"Did Morrison and Hunter have alibis?"

Stone finished his pastry, sat back and sipped his tea.

"Leo Hunter said he dropped off a file to Blackwolf that evening. When I asked what the file was about, he said it had to do with a fishing rights case."

"I'm familiar with it. It was the crux of their conference at the hotel."

"Kelly Morrison told me she talked to the victim around seven. She said it had to do with business."

I wondered if the business was fish or personal.

"May I ask time of death, Sergeant?"

"Between ten and eleven."

"So it was late. Actually, now I remember looking at my clock. When I heard the loud noise it was 10:53 pm."

He nodded. "That might definitely pinpoint the bludgeoning."

"And cause of death?"

"Still undetermined. But from the looks of the deceased, I'd bet it was the blunt force."

CHAPTER SIX

I shuddered at the memory of seeing David Blackwolf lying on the floor.

Sergeant Stone leaned in.

"Here's what I need from you, Mrs. Bradley."

"I hope I can help."

"You had an opportunity to witness the victim and Badger Knight having a heated conversation, as you put it, yesterday."

"That's correct."

"You also attended a meeting and observed the conferees."

"Right."

"Would you be willing to find out what kind of relationships these associates had with Blackwolf? I know it's a huge task, and you're probably here on pleasure, but we have no other leads."

"Do you have anyone particular in mind?"

"Only those you mentioned to me when I first questioned you. I have a list on my phone."

With a deftness that surprised even me, Stone texted the list to my phone:

Kelly Morrison
Badger Knight
Father Goodman
Raymond Crow
Rainbow Knight

Gerald Dawson
Leo Hunter

I studied the list. "I've never met Leo Hunter."

"Doesn't matter. See if you can arrange Kelly Morrison to introduce you. It will seem more natural than if I did."

"This is a tall order and may take some time."

"Mrs. Bradley, after talking to the detectives you've dealt with I'm sure you'll do fine."

I blushed at the compliment.

"We'll do our best."

"Oh, right. I almost forgot you and your dog work as a team."

"Go ahead and make fun. But if there's a clue the police haven't found, Teddy may find it."

Stone checked his phone. "Time to go. Thanks for meeting with me. I have to get back to the station."

"Thanks for the tea. I'd better get busy myself." I smiled, wondering where to start.

Kelly seemed a logical choice. Her feelings for David were obvious.

She loved him. No doubt in my mind.

The next name on the list caused me to swallow hard.

Badger Knight.

What a sour looking man he was! I decided to begin with the worst first and get it over with.

Father Goodman would be a convenient resource to locate most of the individuals Stone asked me to contact. I fished inside my purse for the card he'd given me and called.

"Well, Teddy, you and I have a date with Father Goodman for dinner at his house. What do you think about that?"

"Woof, woof!" Teddy barked.

How he loved the word "dinner."

After freshening up back at the hotel, I checked in with Arthur and Diana and shared my plans for the evening.

They were probably relieved I didn't ask them to dog sit again.

Teddy cocked his head as if he wanted something.

"You're so right, dear doggie. We haven't had a chance to play, have we?"

"Woof!" he barked and perked up his ears.

"Now let me see...where did I put your toys?"

Teddy wagged his stubby tail in anticipation.

"I found them."

Reaching into a special sack, I took out one of his favorites – a stuffed brown ferret which I threw across the room.

"Go get it!" I clapped my hands adding to the fun.

He raced toward the prize as fast as he could, grabbed the toy in his mouth, and marched back to where I stood.

"Give me that ferret." I wrestled it gently from him, then threw it again.

We played fetch until we were exhausted.

I checked the time. "Oh my, we need to call a cab and go see Father Goodman."

Teddy walked to his water dish and lapped.

"I suppose I should feed you before we go."

His tail wagged a "Yes, please."

I took a hotel notepad and stuck it in my purse. It would come in handy to make notes.

After Teddy had eaten his supper, I bent down and gathered him in my arms.

"The driver texted me he's here. Let's get you ready and we'll be off."

After a twenty minute ride answering the proverbial polite questions from the driver, we reached Father Goodman's cheerful looking house.

Painted a cream color with warm apricot trim, the tidy little cottage had a front porch reached by wooden steps that led to the front door. Blooming shrubs and annuals danced around the perimeter.

I knocked.

Barks came from within.

"It appears Father Goodman has a dog and is an avid gardener by the way he keeps his flower beds."

Teddy perked up his ears at the possibility of meeting a new friend and looked around as if he understood my observation.

Soon, the door was opened, and we were greeted by the priest wearing an old orange and yellow flowered apron spattered with various and sundry food.

"Come in, come in." Father Goodman introduced us to his golden retriever. "Francis, this is Jillian and Teddy. Shake hands."

Francis raised a large paw.

I took it gently and gave him a shake. "Nice to meet you, Francis." The dog looked ancient, but Teddy wagged his tail, ready to play.

Father Goodman scooped him up, gave him a hug, and set him on the floor.

With a look of love, the priest explained.

"He's named after St. Francis of Assisi, one of my favorite saints. He's fifteen, Teddy, so go easy on him."

As the older dog walked away, Teddy growled playfully and followed.

"Don't worry, they'll be okay. Francis is patient and used to people. He comes to the office with me most days."

"Teddy," I said, "behave yourself, and no chewing on your new friend."

"Woof!" he barked as if he understood my admonition.

"Your yard is lovely. And something smells wonderful!" I said, sniffing the aroma of beef.

"Thank you. You're lucky I put a pot roast on in the crockpot this morning before I left." He led the way into the kitchen, offered me a seat at the table set for two, and opened the oven door.

"I only need to take the rolls out and we'll be all set."

Teddy raced into the kitchen.

I smiled. "You must smell the pot roast, too."

I pointed next to my chair. "Teddy, sit."

Teddy obeyed on command.

"Good dog."

Father Goodman set our meal on the table. A vintage platter held chunks of succulent beef and vegetables – carrots, potatoes, and onions.

"What a beautiful pattern," I said.

"I inherited it from my grandmother. It's transfer ware."

"Yes. I had a transfer ware pattern years ago. Old Blue Willow is still one of my favorites."

"Not many know the term. Anyway, after she and my mother died, everything came to me since I was the only child. I'll say grace."

We bowed our heads as Father Goodman led the prayer blessing the food. As he offered thanks, I prayed silently that God would lead the conversation.

As we raised our heads, I asked about his family.

"You said you were an only child."

He offered me the platter first. After placing modest amounts of the tender roast and veggies on my plate, he handed me the gravy.

After serving himself, he gave me his full attention.

"I never knew my real parents," he said, "early on, foster parents were all I knew."

"I'm so sorry. I hope it wasn't unpleasant."

"Unpleasant? How about awful? I've forgiven my caregivers, though. Being a foster parent can be unbearably stressful."

The priest's attitude was admirable.

"That's all in the past now. My story did have a happy ending."

I smiled, happy for the man.

"What turned your situation around?"

I took a forkful of succulent pot roast.

MURDER AT THE EMPRESS HOTEL

"An agency worker nurtured my faith. Eventually she had mercy and adopted me as her son. This was in spite of being a single woman who had never married."

"Unusual for those days, I would say."

"Yes it was. Long story short, my adoptive mother gave me her last name of Goodman, paid for my schooling for the priesthood, and gave me enough love to cancel all the bad in my young life."

"What a wonderful story. And you met Father Perkins in seminary, you said."

He nodded and swallowed a mouthful.

After a sip of water he asked, "What about you, Jillian?"

I smiled, wiped the corners of my mouth, and cast my mind back.

"My background was fairly ordinary, which after hearing yours, I can be grateful that it was. Except for losing my first husband Ted in the Vietnam War, and the second man I married dying unexpectedly, my life has been blessed."

The priest closed his eyes a moment, then half smiled. "You have a great attitude."

As the evening drew on we chatted comfortably about ourselves.

I leaned in. "My father was in the Air Force so we lived in many different places. Casablanca for instance. Las Vegas, Albuquerque, New Mexico."

"Lucky you. I would have loved to travel."

"My mother loved it." I said. "I was the oldest of three siblings. My brothers and sister were kind enough to provide me with nieces and nephews. I never had children."

He smiled. "Me neither." We chuckled over the innuendo of his being a priest.

"What brought you to Victoria?" I asked.

He crossed his arms. "While I was in seminary I became interested in religions of ancient peoples, particularly the aboriginals." He uncrossed his arms, sat back, and shared what was obviously the love of his life. "If you have time, I'd love to show you some books I've written on the subject."

"You're published?" I was impressed.

He nodded a little sheepishly. "One thing led to another. When I was given the opportunity to take a position at Royal Roads, I leaped at the chance."

"And here you are. I take it you're also a spiritual advisor."

"You could say that. I prefer to say First Nations calls me their friend."

I reflected on his last statement. It seemed to fit this priest perfectly.

"Now tell me how I can help you, Jillian."

"Sergeant Stone asked if I would talk to those who might have known David Blackwolf. You sprang to mind first as someone who could help."

"I see." He speared the last chunk of carrot on his plate with his fork. "Am I a suspect?"

"As far as I know, there aren't any suspects technically, only persons of interest."

Teddy let out a tiny growl, a reminder that he'd appreciate a bite of beef.

I gave him a tiny morsel.

"Tell me," I asked, "how can I reach Badger Knight?"

"So the police think he's a person of interest?"

I nodded, not wanting to reveal what I knew about the argument.

He shrugged. "Badger and his sister Rainbow live on the reserve. Are you surprised?"

"Yes, as a matter of fact I am. I would think, being a lawyer and a grad student, they'd live in town."

He smiled. "Badger and Rainbow are staunch supporters of First Nation's way of life. They're greatly admired in the community."

"How well do you know them?"

Teddy stretched out under my chair and went to sleep.

"Fairly well."

After we'd eaten our fill, Father Goodman cleared the table and offered dessert.

"Hope you like cheese and fruit." He set dessert plates on the table and a wooden board laden with a white cheese and clusters of grapes.

Teddy poked up his head at the word cheese, then plopped it down again.

"Sounds lovely." I sampled the cheese, which turned out to be a mild Gouda, and popped a few grapes into my mouth.

He shaved a slice of cheese and put it on his plate. "There definitely was bad blood between Badger and David, from a few comments made by Rainbow."

"Do you know how Badger got his limp? I thought it might be the source of his unhappiness."

"You noticed more than his limp, didn't you? Well, you're right. Badger is a defensive young man. I don't think I've ever seen him smile."

"I take it you've known him a long time."

He shook his head this time. "Not really. Rainbow Knight has been my assistant for little over a year. You might say I've been a casual observer."

"That's the way I see myself. Did Rainbow Knight have dealings with David?"

"All I know is they're from the same Songhees Nation. They must be pretty well acquainted."

"I wonder if Raymond Crow might shed some light on Badger. Does he live on the reserve, too?"

"Most definitely, since he's their tribal elder. I do know that he and Badger's father were close. His father was the chief up until his death last year. It is Badger's turn next."

"How tragic for Rainbow and Badger."

He nodded. "Not to sound cliché, but they do believe he went to the happy hunting ground. Many of their people are

Christians, did you know that?"

I shook my head. "I never really thought about it. But I'm glad to hear it in light of a news article I came across recently."

"I think I know the one you're referring to, about the Truth and Reconciliation Commission accusing Canada of cultural genocide?"

"That's the one."

The priest bowed his head then looked up.

"It's amazing to me how God's love can reach hearts of the First Nations who've been horribly mistreated and turn them to forgiveness."

"Amen."

"Here's what I can do." Father Goodman rose and cleared the empty dishes. "Tomorrow morning I'm clear of classes. I'll do my best to arrange for them to meet with you."

"How kind of you. Most helpful. What time should I be ready?"

"Let's say mid-morning. That will give me time to set things up. Our negotiations here are at a standstill anyway."

"Perfect. We really should be going."

I texted the cab to pick me up. "Come along sweet doggie."

Teddy stretched out his paws, and looked at me with sleepy eyes.

"He's well behaved for a terrier." Father Goodman gave him a final pat.

"Teddy can be formidable when he wants. Make no mistake. He's helped find a clue or two on cases I've helped with."

"Now that you mention it, I do recall Father Perkins recounting a story about Teddy saving the day, in Canyon Grove, wasn't it?"

"What a good memory you have."

He smiled at the compliment.

"May I help with the dishes?" I asked.

"Thanks for the offer, but I'm used to cleaning up. Helps me sleep at night."

"If you insist. Thank you for your hospitality. The pot roast was delicious."

"It was my pleasure." As if it was an afterthought, he looked down at the spattered apron. "I forgot to take this off!"

I laughed. "Don't worry, it made me feel at home."

"I'll pick you up at the hotel tomorrow around ten."

"Thanks. Your help is much appreciated. The sooner we find the killer, the better I'll feel. David was murdered next door to my room."

He nodded. "I know."

I didn't recall seeing him at the scene of the crime. Curious.

The cab arrived, Teddy and I climbed in back, and I waved goodbye to Father Goodman standing on the porch.

He looked worried.

CHAPTER SEVEN

Teddy and I reached the hotel and made our way to the fourth floor. My lower back hurt. I wasn't used to walking all day and being out at night. It was time for some pain relievers and a hot bath.

Before filling the tub, I took out a pair of black stretch pants and a cute gray and cream mesh top, perfect for gadding about.

Sitting amongst the fragrant bubbles, allowing the hot water to sooth my sore muscles, I reflected on the evening's conversation with Father Goodman.

If Badger, Rainbow, and David were close, having grown up together with the Songhees, all I had to do was figure out their relationships to one another. Maybe it would shed light on why David was killed, or maybe it wouldn't.

Tomorrow would be a start. It would be best if I could talk to Raymond Crow in private. Somehow, I'd figure out a tactful way to speak to him alone.

I put on a robe.

Teddy was worn out, too. I carried his limp little body to the bed, placed him on his towel, and said goodnight.

Still thinking about what questions to ask tomorrow, I sprayed myself lightly with my favorite scent. After I laid the robe on a chair close to the bed, I crawled beneath the crisp white sheets and turned off the light.

I turned to the window, drapes opened wide, and could

see the harbor shimmering with lights.

Somewhere, a killer lurked. In a hotel room? In an apartment? Or maybe aboard a house boat moored along one of the docks.

What did David do to you that caused you to murder him? I wondered.

As I drifted off to sleep, I tried to picture each person that Sergeant Stone had given me to question who may have had reason to strike David Blackwolf down.

Badger Knight? Definitely. I'd seen him argue with the victim.

Father Goodman? Hard to picture, unless he was trying to protect someone.

Raymond Crow? Perhaps. But would a tribal leader risk losing his position over a single issue?

Rainbow Knight? Yes. She struck me as a person with an iron will.

Leo Hunter? Maybe. But I would have to talk to him first to find out if there was a motive.

The last person I had to talk to was Gerald Dawson. All I could tell so far was that he had an interest in Rainbow. Could be a motive if David was a competitor. It was highly unlikely an educated associate professor would resort to murder, but entirely possible.

That was the problem. Every person on the list could have killed David. I would clearly have to find out why.

Lord, please protect me as I question these people, and guide my thinking. Thank you. Goodnight.

Sleep came instantly. It was morning when I opened my eyes, sunshine filling the room.

"Coffee, Teddy." The pain relievers had worked a little too well. I felt drowsy.

He yawned and stretched, then came to me for snuggles and hugs.

"Good morning."

I dressed, ran a comb through my hair, and touched up

the ends with a curling iron. Simple makeup came last with plenty of moisturizing sunscreen underneath to protect my fair skin.

"Hungry, Teddy?"

He wagged his tail hearing the word. After I set his plate on the floor, filled with his favorites, Teddy devoured everything.

There was plenty of time before my appointment with Father Goodman to meet Arthur and Diana for breakfast in the Gold Lounge to catch up.

With Teddy comfortably situated in his carrier, we found my friends waiting for us, seated on a sofa.

Arthur stood and gave me a hug. Diana smiled and did the same.

"We saved a table near the window." She nodded in the direction of an out-of-the-way space.

"It's perfect." I patted Teddy. "You can sleep while we eat."

We filled our plates with sumptuous slices of ham, fresh fruit, and muffins, then sat together.

The server poured coffee and left.

"Have you read the news?" Arthur asked.

"No. I haven't had a chance."

He handed me his phone queued up to a national news site.

"First Nations Lawyer Slain" read the headline.

"I think they got it wrong. David Blackwolf represented the opposing side."

"Probably capitalizing on the sensationalizing of First Nations." Diana shook her head.

"It's still a mess according to this news report." I sipped my coffee and started to come to life.

"I might as well tell you that Sergeant Stone has asked for my help."

Arthur raised his eyebrows. "Really? I thought the police hated public interference."

"They do. But in this case they have no leads. I happen to be present in the company surrounding him on the day he was murdered. Plus I have credentials."

"If you need any more recommendations," Diana said, "send him to us."

I had to smile.

"It won't be easy. And I apologize ahead of time for not going out with you day tripping."

"Jillian." Arthur covered my hand with his. "We know you'll have far more fun tracking down a killer. Just be careful. You know what happened in Scottsdale when you got too close."

"How could I forget? That's all in the past now. I can't share why I've been asked to help, but when duty calls –."

"We know." Diana looked at Arthur. "Let us know how we can help. If you need us to watch Teddy we'll be happy to."

"Thanks." It was true. I enjoyed helping solve mysteries more than shopping or visiting museums.

"I still want to visit the Butchart Gardens. I'm not leaving until I do!"

"I'm sure you'll get your chance." Arthur checked the time. "Speaking of day tripping, Diana and I have much to see today. Mind if we head out?"

"Not at all. I have an appointment myself at ten. Let's stay in touch and see how the day turns out. I still haven't had afternoon tea here."

Arthur turned to his wife. "Tell you what. Since I don't care a wit about afternoon tea, I'll watch Teddy while you girls imbibe. How's that?"

"He's one in a million, Diana."

She seem to melt as he took her hand. "I know."

"Afternoon tea it is, then."

They waved goodbye as the server refilled my coffee.

With enough caffeine in my system, it was time to meet with Father Goodman.

He was right on time, waiting outside the hotel lobby.

A young man was in the driver's seat.

"Good morning, Jillian. Hop in. This is Gerald Dawson my associate and driver."

One of the suspects on my list!

After securing Teddy in the back seat, Gerald drove us out of town to the reserve.

"I'll let you know when we're ready to leave," Father Goodman said to Gerald.

The first reaction I had seeing the living conditions was great pity. Nothing beyond a few portables and small houses occupied this place, where a once proud people call home.

Father Goodman seemed to read my thoughts.

"Depressing, isn't it? The aboriginals have been summarily eradicated from the face of Canada either by exile or assimilation into the white culture."

"They should have been left alone to live as they see fit. But conquest has been the name of the game throughout history, hasn't it?" I asked, hugging Teddy for comfort.

"I suppose the white man justifies their constant oppression by believing the Indians should become the same as them instead of living the life they've known for centuries."

"And Badger and Rainbow choose to live here in poverty?"

Father Goodman nodded. "They are a strong-willed people. Believe it or not, because of their commitments and leadership from Raymond Crow, the aboriginals are making some strides in being treated fairly and making money."

"That's good to hear."

Up ahead, a long house appeared on the horizon.

"The home of Raymond Crow. We'll talk to him first."

"Perfect."

I was taken by the carvings on the doorposts of Raymond Crow's house. They were not painted as I pictured totem poles in general, but they were interesting.

Father Goodman knocked once.

The door opened immediately. Without a word, Raymond Crow ushered us inside.

Light streamed in from narrow fixed windows near the ceiling. Wood paneling covered the walls, decorated with portraits of chiefs and apparently important tribe members.

"Please sit." Raymond motioned to a sofa covered with a tan slipcover. Father Goodman and I took a seat.

Teddy didn't move as muscle as he sat in my lap.

I wondered if he was frightened.

I thought it best if the priest began.

"As I mentioned before, Jillian has been asked by Sergeant Stone to talk to those who knew David best. She and I have a mutual friend. Father Perkins has shared from firsthand experience what an invaluable resource she can be in a homicide investigation."

Raymond bowed his head. "I am at your service."

On the table behind him, I noticed an unfinished wood project. "Are you a carver?"

He turned to the project. "I am. You must have noticed the family totems on the doorposts."

"I did. I also noticed the one in process. Is it for family?"

He shook his head. "It is a totem of shame." His voice held anger as he spoke.

Father Goodman and I looked at each other.

"We want to hear about it," I said.

Raymond stood and began to pace. "Our people have suffered indignity and shame ever since the white man arrived on our island."

Father Goodman bowed his head. "We understand."

Raymond seemed to appreciate the comment. "Thank you. We were close to a major victory with these negotiations. So close."

"Are you referring to the fishing rights agenda David

was involved with?" I asked.

He nodded. "Only David managed to push through a fishery proposition that would be a huge setback for our people."

"So let me understand," Father Goodman said, "the totem of shame is for David?"

Raymond sat down. "Yes. David was one of us, or half anyway. His mother was of us. By law, she had to leave the tribe if she married outside the tribe."

"But his last name was Blackwolf. That's Indian." I was confused.

"David took his middle name as a way to market himself. I always thought it was two-faced to pretend you're an advocate for your people and then turn your back."

I took out my notepad and a pen. "When did you last see David, Raymond?"

He hung his head. "Truthfully? It was on the night he died."

Father Goodman's mouth dropped, and I was startled at the revelation.

"Tell us what happened. Exactly." I wrote down the name Raymond Crow followed by a colon.

He folded his hands. "After I discovered what David planned to present at the next session, I knew I had to try and talk him out of it."

"So you went to his room? About what time did you go to his room?" I asked.

"It was early. I do know that much. Around seven or seven-thirty, I think. I took our talking stick with me, thinking it would have an impact on the seriousness of what he was about to do."

The stick cruelly protruding from David's body flashed through my memory. Then I remembered seeing it for the first time at the pow wow.

"Do you have the talking stick now?" I asked, hoping

his answer was yes.

He shook his head. "After I pleaded with him, he refused to retract his proposal. I was so angry that I pushed him against the wall and left."

"And you left the stick in his room?" Father Goodman asked.

"Yes, my great anger caused me to forget. It was irresponsible of me to leave something so important."

This wasn't good for Raymond.

"What time did you leave?" I asked.

"I didn't stay long. I left before eight and came home."

"Can anyone corroborate that?" I asked.

He thought a moment. "No. I live alone. It wasn't until I heard the news report the next morning that I learned David was dead."

I finished writing down the details. "What can you tell me about the relationship between Badger Knight and David?"

Raymond Crow smiled.

CHAPTER EIGHT

The proud tribal elder stood. "I have been a bad host. The story of Badger and David may take some time. You will need a cup of tea."

Father Goodman and I had no objections.

The long house was constructed as an open space, originally designed with built in beds along each inner wall. Raymond made his way to the kitchen space, set a kettle of water to boil on top of the stove, and took out three mismatched mugs from a rustic cabinet next to the small sink.

The priest and I sat quietly and waited until the kettle whistled. Teddy perked up his ears but continued to sit in my lap patiently.

I stroked his fur to reassure him in his strange surroundings filled with tribal antiquities and smells of numerous animal pelts.

Raymond handed us our tea. "I apologize if you use sugar. I do not keep it."

Oh, well. I usually take three, but in this case, straight would have to do.

"No," I said. "This will be fine for me."

Father Goodman took a mug. "Thanks."

"Badger, Rainbow, and David grew up together here on the reserve. At least they often played together. David's mother and Badger and Rainbow's mother were sisters."

I took a sip of the strong green tea. "So they were

MURDER AT THE EMPRESS HOTEL

cousins?"

"In a sense. I must clarify what I mean by sisters. The two women were close as sisters. When Rainbow's mother died in childbirth, David's mother stepped in to care for her. She did so even though they lived outside the tribe."

"I see," Father Goodman said "Due to his father not being part of the tribe."

"Correct. They lived close enough, though, to see each other often. David's father was a doctor, and that brings me to the story."

We sat back and listened, sipping our tea.

"One day, when the three children were playing on a ledge down by the creek, Badger slipped and fell headfirst into the water, knocking him out. If it hadn't been for David, he would have drowned."

Now dawned a possible reason for Badger's angry countenance.

"What did Rainbow do?" I asked.

"David told her to run for help. I happened to be one of the ones who carried him back home."

I pictured the whole thing in my mind. Badger the victim, David the hero. Rainbow caught in the middle.

"Go on, what happened after you got him home?"

"David's father came to help set Badger's broken leg. Badger had suffered a concussion as well."

Father Goodman shook his head. "Obviously, by Badger's limp, the leg didn't set correctly."

Raymond nodded. "Badger never forgave David's father for making him a cripple. From then on, there was animosity between the two boys."

I set my tea on the small table in front of us. "It must have been difficult for Rainbow, especially since David's mother was looking after her."

"Difficult? It was impossible. She finally couldn't take the hateful looks and stabbing words Badger threw at her, and had to quit."

"Who cared for Rainbow after that happened?"

After a pause, Raymond said, "I did."

I was astounded.

He continued. "There was always rivalry between the two boys, before the accident and especially after it happened. Badger's spirit grew dark while David's spirit seemed to flourish."

Father Goodman was well into the story by now. "Tell us how they became lawyers."

"When David's father saw to it that his son had every advantage including law school, I helped Badger's father garner community support for Badger to do the same."

"You and the chief were close?" I asked.

Raymond smiled for the second time. "We were brothers, by blood. Even though he has passed from this life, his spirit is still with me."

The closeness he felt for him was touching.

"It was difficult to put Badger through school." He continued. "Many sacrifices were made, including some of his own. Badger was an exemplary student and worked to pay for expenses."

"You were proud of him, weren't you?"

Raymond nodded. "Extremely proud. Especially when he represented us so brilliantly."

Father Goodman took out his phone, typed a text, and stood. "I wish we could stay longer, but I have a class to teach this afternoon and need to get Jillian home."

I placed Teddy on the floor to stretch before putting him in his tote.

"Raymond, thank you for seeing us this morning. You've helped with good insight."

"It's an honor to have you in my home, Jillian."

I stuffed Teddy in his carrier. Father Goodman held the door open for us as we stepped outside to wait for Gerald.

Raymond didn't walk us out. When we left, he still sat in his chair, staring at the floor.

After we settled in the car, I turned to Father Goodman. "That was quite an interview."

"I agree. Are you thinking what I'm thinking?"

"If you're thinking Raymond Crow doesn't have an airtight alibi, then yes."

"No. I was thinking about motive. Raymond is protective not only of his people, but Badger."

"Go on."

"What if Raymond tries to talk David out of his damaging proposal because it will bring shame to Badger's defense?"

"Sort of an underlying motive since Raymond worked so hard getting Badger to where he is."

"Yes. David won't back away so Raymond gets mad and kills him."

Gerald glimpsed in the rear view mirror at Father Goodman.

"It's possible," I said. "How can I get hold of Badger?"

"I'll have Rainbow set it up. She'll be there today after my class."

"You're an angel! There's the hotel, we're here."

Gerald pulled in front of the hotel, got out of the car, and helped me out with Teddy.

"I'll call you after I talk to Rainbow," Father Goodman said.

"Thanks for everything today."

"It'll cost you. I have a few garden questions."

We chuckled.

"Come along, Teddy. We'll take a quick walk before lunch as soon as we get back to the hotel."

He perked up his ears and panted at the mention of a walk.

I didn't relish the idea of eating alone. The Gold Lounge only served breakfast and appetizers so I was out of luck there.

On the way to a walking path, I had an idea.

"Teddy, I think I'll touch base with Sergeant Stone and see if he's free for lunch. It might not hurt to catch up."

He answered after the second ring.

"Mrs. Bradley. It's nice to hear from you. Do you have anything for me?"

"Maybe. May I buy you lunch?"

There was a slight pause.

"You're in luck. I was about to go out for a bite."

"You're the expert. Where shall we meet?"

"You say you're buying?"

"Correct."

"We could try Jam Café. Sometimes there's a queue but I have an hour for lunch."

"I'll meet you there. Grab a table if you arrive first. Teddy will be along so hopefully we can eat outside."

"I'll see what I can do. Meet you in a bit."

A long line stretched in front of the popular eating establishment. I checked the desk to find out if Sergeant Stone was successful getting a table.

"Yes, ma'am. We're accommodating your service dog." He nodded toward the back where Sergeant Stone awaited.

"Thank you." I made my way through the crowded café, taking note of the fabulous plates of food.

Teddy sniffed the air in anticipation.

"Have a seat." Stone motioned to the chair across the table from where he sat.

"Service dog?" I whispered.

"As far as I'm concerned, he is."

After settling Teddy beside my chair, the server approached.

He handed us menus, took our drink orders and soon returned with tall glasses of ice water.

"What can I get for you?" he asked.

Sergeant Stone deferred to me.

It was a toss-up between the caramel banana pancakes and the eggs Benedict until I noticed a Rueben. "I'll have the Reuben Benny." Reubens in any form were my favorite.

"And I'll have the Oscar Benedict."

I noticed his choice included a flat iron steak and asparagus. It was tempting.

"I'm anxious to hear what you've found out." Stone took a sip of water, then gave his full attention.

"So far I've talked to Kelly, Father Goodman, and Raymond Wolf. I get the sense that Kelly was in love with David, but I'm not sure it was reciprocated."

"That's a good start. Go on."

"When Father Goodman and I had dinner together, the only thing I learned was he's worried about something…or someone."

"And Raymond Crow?"

The server returned with huge plates of food and set them down.

Teddy poked up his nose and sniffed.

"Don't worry, sweet doggie, I'll give you a bite." I handed him a prime morsel of the meat.

"Now, back inside your carrier and go to sleep."

He was reluctant to obey.

After I sampled the dish I completely understood. It was incredible!

"Raymond Crow offered the most information so far. Unfortunately for him, he doesn't have an airtight alibi. He did go to David's room that night and they argued, pretty heavily."

"I see. What was the argument about?"

I took another bite of Montreal smoked beef and sauerkraut before answering.

"Fishing rights. Evidently, David was postured to present an interloper to the First Nations fishing grounds that would further diminish their territory."

"I believe Raymond Crow would definitely get upset over that."

"He told me that he became angry enough to push David

against the wall."

Breaking my "eat only half portion" rule to control my weight, I ate the rest of my lunch.

After wiping the corners of my mouth with my napkin, I placed my fork across the empty plate.

"Sergeant, the awful thing I have to tell you is that the murder weapon belonged to Raymond."

CHAPTER NINE

At first, Stone looked surprised before nodding. "If that's the case, why would he leave it as evidence against himself?"

"I wondered the same thing. Unless he told us the truth about going to see David, arguing, and leaving infuriated, causing him to forget taking it with him."

"It could have happened that way."

When the server returned, I paid the check.

"Father Goodman is setting up an appointment with Rainbow Knight. If I learn anything important I'll let you know."

Stone looked thoughtful. "This case is quite a puzzle. So far, all our leads have come to a dead end. It reminds me of one I've been trying to solve for years."

The mystery unfolded as this man reached back in his memory and recounted the details of the murder.

As he told me his story, he took out the sack of red cinnamon candy, again.

I cocked my head and asked a silent question.

"If you're wondering why I eat, it's because I want to constantly remind myself to keep awake until I solve this case. Cinnamon does it for me."

"I did wonder. So, what happened?" I sat back to listen.

"A woman was found murdered in Dragon Ally, not too far from here, in fact. There was no evidence, not even a name. We call her Jane Doe."

"Sad. How did she die?"

"Some sort of blunt trauma to the head. Her face was unrecognizable. We tried to investigate, but no one filed a missing person's report."

"Strange. How long ago did it happen?"

Sergeant Stone shook his head. "It's been several years, almost too long to remember."

"And no leads in all that time?"

Again, he shook his head.

"It happened when I was partners with a rookie. We were on his first routine patrol when he pointed to some suspicious activity in Dragon Alley."

"That's in Chinatown?"

"Yeah. A crowd had gathered around something." He shuddered. "It was our Jane Doe."

"Anyway, after we pulled over I let the rookie make the call. He was so nervous that he called the wrong number. It distracted me from the scene trying to help him. "

"Oh dear. That was bad, wasn't it?"

"By the time he alerted dispatch, a significant crowd had gathered and contaminated any evidence in the area."

Stone shut his eyes a moment, then looked somewhere in the distance.

"Rest assured, though, I'm not giving up finding her killer. It's the only case I haven't solved."

Teddy began to squirm.

"I'm sorry, but I need to get Teddy outside."

A smile crossed Stone's face. "I'm ready."

We came outside into the balmy air. "Do you need a lift back to the hotel?" Stone asked checking his watch.

"Thanks for the offer, but you should get back. I'll call a cab after I take Teddy for a walk."

He saluted in a joking manner. "Thanks for lunch, Jillian. And your help."

As we parted ways, I attached Teddy's leash, set him on the sidewalk, and searched for a patch of grass.

Trees were plentiful along the sidewalks. Soon Teddy found a spot, and we paused.

From the looks of the neighborhood, we were close to Chinatown. Tourists crowded the streets and slowed traffic.

Not too far from where we stood I looked across the way. I could read one street sign – Dragon Ally.

My heart sank at the thought of Stone's Jane Doe losing her life only steps from where Teddy and I had stopped.

Lord, please help Sergeant Stone find her killer.

As I ended my prayer, Father Goodman sent a text: *Rainbow available until three this afternoon.*

I answered:

Thanks. On our way.

I scooped up Teddy, put him in his carrier and hailed a cab.

"Royal Roads University."

"Yes, ma'am." The driver started the counter.

We were on our way.

Red and white Canadian flags bearing the maple leaf fluttered along the streets of downtown as we drove.

Baskets of hanging pelargonium, petunias and impatiens hung outside the quaint shops and restaurants, brightening the landscape.

Victoria was a garden lover's paradise. I ached to see the Butchart Gardens.

All in good time, I told myself.

Royal Roads University was a twenty minute ride from our current location. It felt good to sit and enjoy the views of the lush green landscape along the Trans-Canada Highway.

What I hadn't realized was the university is located on the largest National Historic Site in Canada. Royal Roads is the tenant and maintains and oversees the daily workings of the estate.

Hatley Park turned out to be a 565 acre Edwardian estate built for local coal baron James Dunsmuir. I looked up the details on my phone and read that, besides the university, the grounds encompass the original mansion, carefully preserved old-growth forest, and miles of trails.

Several acres of manicured gardens caught my attention immediately.

"How lovely!" I exclaimed to the driver.

"Indeed they are, ma'am. You'll want to visit the Japanese gardens as well as the Rose and Italian ones. There's a fee, but you may find it's well worth it."

"You can drop us off at the Blue Heron House. It's next to the Boat House from what I was told."

"Sure. It overlooks Esquimalt Lagoon."

The driver pulled up to a two-storied long house built of wood.

I was struck by the similarity to Raymond Crow's home.

"I'll give you a call if I need a ride back." I paid the driver, hooked the leash onto Teddy, and we got out of the car.

An eagle soared overhead, and we watched it land in a nest held high in a tree.

"That's something you don't see every day," I said halfway under my breath. When I turned, Father Goodman stood by the front door to greet us.

"Rainbow wanted to meet here. It's out of the way and quiet."

"Can't believe we saw an eagle."

"This lagoon is a bird sanctuary. The indigenous students chose the name of Blue Heron House since the name Blue Heron means community."

"How appropriate. I'm beginning to understand how special their culture is."

He smiled and opened the door for us.

Once inside, I observed the old mixed with the new. A colorful Indian rug anchored the inviting living room which had a view of the lagoon.

Rainbow stood to greet us, then had us sit close together.

At first I didn't recognize her in street clothes. With her dark hair flowing loose instead of braids, she was even lovelier.

It was a blessing to find ourselves alone in the student services building.

"Thanks for meeting with me," I said.

There was a sadness about her, much more than the serious aura I'd encountered when we first met.

"I'm so sorry about David," I said.

"Thank you. His death doesn't seem real. And yet my spirit feels as if part of me is gone."

"I understand. You were close friends?"

"We were in love."

Father Goodman and I exchanged shocked looks.

"I'm truly sorry for your loss." I paused for words. "Rainbow, can you tell us how long you were in a relationship? It's important for us to know as much about David as we can to find out who killed him." Father Goodman had asked the question for me.

"I suppose David and I always knew we'd be together one day. I can't explain how we knew. It was more of an understanding."

"This understanding." I couldn't help thinking about what Kelly's relationship had been. "Who knew about it?"

Rainbow bowed her head. "No one."

"No one?" I was confused.

"If Badger had even had the slightest suspicion he would have forbidden me to even talk to David."

"So you met secretly." Father Goodman nodded in a kindly way. "I sensed something wasn't right these past few days. Now I know it was you and David."

"We wanted to tell everyone, but David insisted on making his peace with Badger first."

"When did you last see David?" I asked.

Rainbow shifted in her seat. "It was on the night he was killed."

Tears filled her eyes.

"It was late – around nine-thirty when I arrived. David said he had a few appointments and had to finish a file before he was free to see me."

"Did he say with whom?"

She shook her head. "No, wait. I remember noticing our tribal talking stick on the coffee table. When I asked what it was doing there, he said Raymond Crow must have forgotten to take it with him earlier in the evening."

I caught Father Goodman's eye. We must have thought the same thing. Raymond Crow was telling the truth.

"Can you think of anyone else he may have talked to that night?" I asked.

"There was one odd thing that happened, now that I think about it."

I leaned in. "Go on."

"It happened soon after I arrived. There was a knock at the door. David got up to see who it was, and looked through the peephole. He cracked the door open, but only slightly."

"So you didn't see who it was."

She shook her head again, and frowned.

"I heard him say, 'come back later.' Then he shut the door and came back into the living room."

Father Goodman shrugged. "Perhaps it was housekeeping. Sometimes they offer a turn down service."

"Would you care for some tea?" Rainbow asked.

She seemed nervous talking about David's death.

"I'd love some." I reached over to pat Teddy settled beside me.

"Thanks, Rainbow," Father Goodman said.

"I'll only be a moment."

After she left the room, I turned to Father Goodman.

"Don't you find it curious that if it was housekeeping who paid the late night call, David would have simply mentioned it?"

"A valid point."

Rainbow returned with steaming mugs of tea on a small tray. "Sugar?"

"I'll take three, please," I said.

She stirred in three packets, and handed me the stone mug.

"Father Goodman?" she asked.

"None for me, thanks." He patted his generous girth. "I have to watch my calories."

We all smiled at his little joke.

"Rainbow, is there anything else you can tell us about that night?" I asked.

"Aside from sitting together on the couch, cradled in his arms, talking about our life together, it was as if we were the only two people in the world."

Her words caused me to reflect on how my husband and I felt the same way when we first fell in love.

"Can you remember anything about the room, what you ate or drank, or any other details?"

"I'm trying to remember." She folded her hands, and laid them in her lap.

"We didn't eat or drink anything. There was no need."

Again, I understood.

Father Goodman blushed.

Teddy stretched and gave a little sigh.

"It was a beautiful night." Rainbow looked out with haunting eyes. "David had the window open. That's all I can remember right now. I hope I was able to help," Rainbow said.

"I may want to talk to you again, if you wouldn't mind," I said.

"No, anything I can do."

She reached inside her purse, took out a piece of paper and a pen, and scribbled her phone number.

"Here. Call me whenever you want."

"Thanks."

As we stood to leave, Father Goodman's driver walked in and hailed us.

Gerald Dawson was someone I needed to talk to.

CHAPTER TEN

Rainbow looked uneasy as she joined our group.

She uncrossed her legs, shifted her position, and smoothed a non-existent wrinkle on her slacks.

Teddy wagged his tail as if hoping for attention.

"Hey, little guy." Gerald reached to pat the happy pup. "Stopped by to see if anyone needed a lift home."

Gerald looked at Rainbow as he spoke.

"Hi, Gerry Berry," she said.

He blushed at being called the nickname.

"Thanks," Rainbow said, "but I have my car. Father Goodman and I have some work to do before we leave. I'll take him home."

It was a perfect opportunity to ask for a ride.

I raised my hand. "I could use one back to my hotel. If you're going that way."

He looked away from Rainbow and patted Teddy again.

"Sure. I live right across the street."

Father Goodman and Rainbow stood.

"Gerald has a houseboat, in case you're wondering, Jillian," the priest said.

"Really? I was admiring them as we arrived. I'd love to know how it would be to live on the water."

"At the moment, it means doing repairs. The boat's not much, but I'm getting there. At least it doesn't leak anymore." Gerald spoke directly to Rainbow.

His love for her was obvious.

I wondered if she knew.

"I'm sure you'll make it livable one day," Rainbow said. She turned to Father Goodman.

"I'm ready to get back to work whenever you are."

Gerald shuffled his feet. "Rainbow, I'm...I'm sorry about David."

Rainbow lowered her eyes. "Thank you."

"Is there anything I can do?" Gerald asked. "I'm here for you."

She smiled. "I know. Right now I need time alone."

He nodded. "I'll see you at work, then."

She barely nodded.

Before she left she turned to me. "Find whoever killed David."

"I'll do my best."

Father Goodman bid goodbye to Teddy with a final pat.

"I'll catch a ride with Rainbow. See you soon, Jillian. Take care."

He had the same serious look as when we said our goodbyes after dinner at his house – what was he hiding?

"Shall we?" Gerald asked. "May I carry Teddy for you?"

"Thanks."

Teddy wagged his tail at having someone new to investigate with his nose.

Gerald chuckled as Teddy sniffed his face.

His car was parked nearby, thankfully, so I didn't have to walk far. I was beginning to feel a little arthritis in my leg after gadding about.

All was quiet except for the crunching of gravel beneath our feet until a whoosh from overhead caused us to look up.

Two bald eagles soared above, winging their way to a nest on top of a tall distant pine.

It was an unforgettable moment.

Teddy perked up his ears in Gerald's arms as if fascinated with the huge birds.

"I'm glad you had a chance to see our local royalty."

Gerald opened the door for me.

After we settled in for the ride I started the conversation, hoping to find out his moves the night of the murder.

"How did you hear about David?" I asked.

As if snapping from a day dream, he replied.

"Oh, I saw the police cars when I came home from a second job I have and asked a bystander what it was all about."

"That's right – you live directly across from where it happened."

So much for opportunity. Gerald admitted being at the scene.

"What's your second job?" I asked.

"I lead one of the ghostly walks here in Victoria. They're quite popular with tourists."

"Yes, I've read about them. What time did you get home?"

"Must have been around 11 pm. That's usually the time I get home."

"David Blackwolf was killed minutes before. Did you speak to anyone?"

He shook his head. "Only a stranger."

I decided to take a chance and probe.

"How long have you known Rainbow?"

A smile broke across his face.

"I met her at the university at the beginning of the year. Why do you ask?"

"Forgive a personal question but are you in love with her?"

Gerald grew serious, more serious than I'd ever seen him.

"Is it that obvious?"

"Maybe only to me. Forgive my forthrightness, but have you told her?"

Again, he shook his head.

"I haven't had the nerve. Then I saw them together.

After the way she looked at David, the way I wish she'd look at me, I figured I didn't have a chance."

"When was this?"

He considered. "It was at the last meeting. When David spoke her eyes were riveted on him. As he took a seat I watched him give her a smile."

"So that's when you knew they were in a relationship."

"Yeah, that's when I knew."

We'd reached the bridge, drawing closer to the hotel. I only needed a little more time.

"Did you ever visit Raymond Crow in his home?"

Gerald cast a sideways glance.

"Yes. Once. I interviewed him as part of the research on my thesis "The Golden Age of Aboriginals.""

Now I was convinced Gerald knew about the talking stick.

Since my prying had obviously been painful, I steered the conversation away from Rainbow and David Blackwolf and asked about the houseboat.

"You can't actually maneuver the boat out of the harbor, can you? The ones I saw looked permanent."

"Most of them are." He smiled. "I do have a small boat, though, parked in the marina. I plan to travel one of these days."

I smiled, picturing Gerald sailing off to adventure.

"Here's the hotel." He pulled in front, parked, and came around to help me out.

"Thank you. You're a true gentleman."

"Woof," Teddy barked.

Gerald gave him a final pat.

"Let me know if you ever need a lift. I'm right across the street."

He handed me his card.

"And if you're really curious about who killed Blackwolf, talk to Badger Knight."

He smiled as he left.

I couldn't help but finding him likable.

Please don't let him be the killer, I thought. Yet he did have motive, means, and opportunity.

And no alibi.

I dreaded talking to Badger. He seemed so impersonal and angry. It may be a good idea to talk to him with Rainbow present, to protect myself in case.

I'd call her in the morning. Right now, all I wanted was to take Teddy for a walk, rest a little, and have something to eat.

A text from Arthur popped up on my phone:

Join us for dinner? Will wait for your answer.

I texted back:

Just got home. Will come to your room after I take Teddy for a walk and rest a few minutes. Thanks!

It would be nice to have company for dinner.

Teddy and I took a brief walk suggested by the hotel where he could sniff to his heart's delight. He lowered his ears when he saw we were alone.

"Okay, sweet doggie. After you've finished we'll go back to the room and play a little fetch. I know you need some one-on-one. I'll get you some food, too."

"Woof," he barked when he heard some of his favorite words.

Once inside the room I slipped off my shoes, and we played fetch with his favorite stuffed blue pig until he began to pant.

"That's enough for now. Let's get you some fresh water and some food. Then I'm going to lie down a few minutes."

After a meal of ground turkey, veggies, and wild rice (one of his favorites), I took a short nap with Teddy. We were both tuckered out.

I changed into a fresh outfit for the evening – a long white skirt, rhinestone studded T-shirt, and a jean jacket, popped Teddy into his tote, and headed for the Wingate's room.

"Jillian!" Diana welcomed me when I arrived. She was stunning in an aqua tunic straight from Scottsdale over white slacks. "Come in and tell us about your day."

"Hello, my dear." Arthur kissed me on the cheek. "You're glowing with information – I can always tell."

He made me blush.

"Is it that obvious? Guess I wouldn't make a good poker player."

We all chuckled.

"I'll tell you over dinner. Where are we going?"

"Depends on what you're hungry for." Diana looked at Arthur. "Doesn't matter to me."

"What about salmon? That's what all the fuss is about here, isn't it?" I said.

"I've heard of a place on the waterfront." Arthur reached for his phone. "It's supposed to have fabulous views of the waterfront and a great menu. We'll head there."

He looked at Teddy. "I'll call ahead and make sure Teddy can get in."

"Thanks, Arthur. I appreciate it." I stroked my little companion. "I won't leave you in the room, I promise."

Teddy panted as if to say, "Thanks, Mistress."

What an intelligent little dog he was. A good judge of character, too. Not always, but he could look on the heart, of that I was certain.

"All set." Arthur clicked off his phone. "I will call a cab for Aura. I've reserved a patio seating."

"Sounds perfect!" Diana grabbed her purse. "Shall we head for the lobby?"

CHAPTER ELEVEN

The view from our restaurant was nothing short of spectacular.

At night, Victoria twinkled as if it were a fairyland with colorful illuminations reflecting in the harbor against a black sky.

White lights boldly outlined the Parliament Buildings.

On either side of its entrance, the Empress was brightly lit with red. With green ivy covered walls it was almost as if the grand hotel was decorated for Christmas.

Our meal was pleasant. I hadn't realized Aura was high end Pacific Rim Asian food. The only thing on the menu that had appealed was the Peking-spice rubbed duck breast with ginger puree, balsamic roasted broccoli, roasted peanuts, sour cherry gastrique (whatever that was), and sesame seeds.

We chatted about the sights Arthur and Diana visited during the day. As we dined, I couldn't help but think about the night David was murdered.

"Jillian," Diana said, "You look a million miles away. Tell us what's on your mind."

I lay down my fork, tempted to offer Teddy a teeny bite of freshly grilled duck. Some restaurant's frowned on feeding dogs on their premises, so I refrained.

"Forgive me, Diana. I can't help wondering about the night David Blackwolf was killed. It must have been a night similar to this one. Yet something triggered a rage that resulted in murder."

"What have you learned? Anything?" Arthur sipped his wine then dabbed his mouth with his cloth napkin.

"A little. I've spent time with Father Goodman who looks worried about something. I don't know if it's in regards to Rainbow Knight or her brother Badger Knight."

"Have you talked to them?" Diana sat back after finishing her entrée.

"I haven't talked to Badger yet. I'm not looking forward to the confrontation."

"Why is that?" Arthur asked.

"Badger Knight has a dark sense about him. He's angry and defensive. I'm asking Rainbow to go with me when I talk to him."

"Sounds wise to me." Arthur smiled. "Anyone for dessert?"

Diana and I shook our heads.

"Then I'll be good, too." Arthur patted his flat stomach.

After I'd eaten half of my duck, I asked the server to box up the leftovers for Teddy later.

On the way home I wanted to share about the talking stick and Raymond Crow's leaving it in David's room but decided against divulging information. Sergeant Stone wouldn't appreciate it.

We'd reached the hotel. Once inside, I reached for my key.

"Dinner was delightful. Thanks for inviting me."

"You have a standing invitation, Jillian." Diana hugged me. "Have a good night."

Once inside our room I took Teddy out and hugged him.

"I love you, sweet dog." I kissed his little head. "Let's go for one last walk after I make a call and then head for bed."

He perked up his ears at the word "walk."

"Woof, woof!" he barked clearly in favor of my suggestion.

I took the slip of paper Rainbow had given me and called the number.

It wouldn't be easy arranging an appointment with her defiant brother, but I had to try.

"Rainbow?" I said when she answered.

"It's Jillian, isn't it?"

"Yes. I need a favor."

"Anything."

"Would you arrange for us to meet with Badger – say over lunch tomorrow – I need to talk to him."

"Sure. Badger loves to eat. Tell me where and when, and I'll make sure we're there."

"Any time and any place you suggest. You know the area better than I do."

"Okay. Give me your email. I'll text you, if that's agreeable."

"Perfect. I'll see you tomorrow."

That went well. The hard part would be talking to Badger face to face.

All I could think about was soaking in a lovely hot bubble bath and getting ready for bed. But Teddy's walk came first.

When we were finally back to our room, I quickly removed his leash and gave him a nice brushing.

"There. Now you look dashing!"

He wagged his tail as if agreeing with me.

"Up you go," I said putting him on his towel.

He wanted to sniff the chocolate that housekeeping left on my pillow for the turn down service.

"No chocolate for dogs. I'm sorry." I took a small treat from my doggie bag and tossed it to him. "This will have to do."

But I can have chocolate!

I unwrapped the truffle, popped it into my mouth, and ran a bath.

While the tub filled, I recalled what Rainbow had said at

Raymond Crow's house.

"It was a beautiful night." Rainbow had looked out with haunting eyes. *"David had the window open. That's all I can remember right now."*

Anyone could have bludgeoned David and exited through the window.

Tomorrow I would take a closer look.

A spray of perfume on my throat and wrists, a quick brush through my hair, and I was ready for bed.

I laid out an outfit for the next day, turned off the light, and climbed wearily into bed.

As I lay back on the soft pillow my mind was in a whirl.

Lord, please help me to think clearly about all the information I gather. I want Rainbow and Kelly to find peace about who killed David. Amen.

Unable to sleep with all the events of the past few days, I tried focusing on each suspect I'd talked to, sorting out motive, means, and opportunity.

Kelly Morrison had loved David. It was difficult to picture her hitting him with the talking stick and stabbing him in a brutal manner.

Still, she admitted being in his room that evening. I needed to find out where she was the rest of the evening.

Father Goodman would be the last person I'd suspect of murder – unless his motive was strong enough. He was protective of Rainbow, of that I was sure.

Gerald Dawson was in love with Rainbow. Would he kill Blackwolf to level the competition?

No. I didn't believe he would. For Gerald's level of intelligence it would take a stronger motive to kill.

Raymond Crow had motive, means, and opportunity. It was hard to believe he'd leave a telling murder weapon at the scene. It didn't fit.

Only two more suspects to talk to. Leo Hunter would be hard to pin down unless Kelly could set up an appointment.

I'd save Leo for last.

"Better turn off your brain and get some sleep, Jillian. Talking to Badger Knight tomorrow will be a challenge."

I closed my eyes.

All I could see was Badger's angry face.

When I awoke the next morning Teddy was stretching at the foot of the bed. He yawned and let out a small unintelligible sound.

"Good morning, little sweet thing."

Teddy wagged his tale and pranced to where I lay.

"You don't mind me calling you sweet thing since you're a boy, do you? After all you are the smartest and handsomest Yorkie I know!"

"Woof!" he barked as if in total agreement.

"Come on." I gathered him in my arms and slid out of bed. "We have a full day today. Better pray an extra prayer over our meeting with Badger Knight and his sister."

Teddy growled.

I smiled.

"So you have an opinion of him, too, I see."

Teddy wagged his tail and licked my cheek.

Before my feet hit the floor I prayed.

Lord, please go before me today and open the door to Badger's heart. Amen.

"There. I feel better now. I'll make your breakfast after I throw on some clothes and take you for a...."

I stopped before uttering the word to give myself a little more time to wake up.

Teddy cocked his head as if understanding part of the sentence.

"Oh, you're clearly too smart for your own good!"

I had to chuckle as I gave him a hug.

Sunshine streamed into the room with a promise of another gorgeous day. The window beckoned.

Placing my hands on the frame, I raised it open with no effort. A flashback of David's room caused me to remember his window was open when I found him.

The murderer must have left that way.

When I looked outside I found a ledge, decorative yes, but wide enough to stand on. I would find out if Stone had done any forensic research outside.

I needed coffee!

Dressed in a nice navy sweat suit, I put a leash on Teddy and got a cup to go in the Gold Lounge.

"Time for our walk, old boy."

Teddy perked up his ears and wagged his tail. He was ready!

Outside, as we walked along the quaint streets filled with hanging baskets, I peered into shop windows and restaurants and became a tourist, enjoying Victoria at a leisurely pace.

We passed a few street musicians lending a festive mood.

Many were tourists, like me, but I suspected residents of Victoria were also enjoying the amenities of this beautiful harbor city.

I inhaled the air filled with aromas of cooking mingled with the smell of the sea.

"Teddy, we need to go back now. We need to eat."

He stopped in his tracks at the mention of a meal, perked up his ears, and pawed my leg.

"You want me to carry you, right?"

"Woof!" he barked.

I picked him up and carried him back to the room.

By the time Teddy had finished his meal, I had dressed for the day.

"You can nap in your carrier while I eat."

Off we went to the Gold Lounge, where I enjoyed another succulent array of pastries, fruit and cheese.

As I finished the last bite of a cheese Danish, a text from Rainbow buzzed on my phone:

Will have to meet at the police station. Badger's been arrested!

I swallowed hard, left a tip, and took Teddy into the hall.

Stone had to be contacted immediately.

"There wasn't much I could do," he said. "Badger Knight fits the profile perfectly as having killed Blackwolf."

"What proof do you have?"

"We have your eye witness of them arguing for one."

"And?"

"They had a history of animosity, not only in their profession but in their personal lives as well."

"So why did you ask for my help? It sounds as if you went out and got what you wanted on your own."

Silence.

"Don't get so upset, Jillian. Think about it. What if he is the killer? Better to get him behind bars so he won't harm anyone else."

Now there was silence on my end.

"It sounds as if you've made up your mind. Rainbow set up a time for me to talk to him today. Any chance?"

"We'll be listening on the other side."

CHAPTER TWELVE

I took Stone's comment as a yes. "Okay," I said. "I'll be there as soon as I can get a cab. And thank you."

My hands shook, but I managed to hail a cab outside.

"Police station, please."

The driver raised his eyebrows then turned on the counter.

"Yes, ma'am."

Even Teddy was trembling.

"Don't worry, we'll have to trust The Lord in this."

With Teddy slung over my shoulder in his soft carrier, the desk sergeant led us to Stone's office.

Rainbow rose from a chair and fell into my arms.

"Badger didn't kill David. You have to help him, Jillian! Please!"

"There, there." I patted her gently. "Everything will be all right. I'm going to do my best to get him freed."

Stone lowered his head. "I'm afraid that's going to be difficult."

"And why is that?" I asked.

"Knight admitted he killed him."

I was stunned, along with Rainbow, whose expression suggested this was the first she'd heard, too.

"Sergeant, I still need to talk to him."

Stone shuffled some paperwork on his desk and shrugged.

"I'll give you 15 minutes. Then I am going to book

him."

"Thank you."

"I'm coming, too," Rainbow said.

I nodded. "He'll need your support."

Sergeant Stone led the way to a holding room, unlocked the door, and told the presiding officer he could leave.

"We'll be watching," Stone said as Rainbow and I entered the cheerless space.

Badger rose from his chair and embraced his sister.

"Jillian is here to help us. Badger, why did you admit to something you didn't do? Why?"

He hung his head.

"I don't think he killed anyone." I took a seat across from where he had been sitting.

After he sat again he sighed.

"It's a long story. And it's better this way. That's all I'm going to say with them listening."

We turned to the two way mirror where Stone and others were observing.

"I understand." I took Teddy out and placed him in my lap. "People usually do anything to protect those they love."

Badger looked at Rainbow.

"That's what I thought," I said. Badger was only trying to shield his sister.

Rainbow grew angry and pushed her brother.

Teddy cowered, afraid.

"You think I killed David? Are you insane? Why would you think such a terrible thing?"

He shook his head.

"Badger," I said gently, "will you talk to me if it's in private? Off the record?"

Rainbow cried.

"I love you Badger, and I loved David. I don't want to lose you, too! Do you understand?"

He hugged her.

"Okay," he whispered to me. "I'll talk to you in private, lady."

Stone entered the room.

"It will have to be in a cell if you want privacy. I'm sorry, but that's my protocol. Rainbow will have to keep Teddy while you talk."

"Be a good dog, Teddy." I was reluctant to leave him but had no choice. I handed him to her along with the tote.

"Don't worry, Jillian. He'll be fine with me."

Another officer led us to where Badger would be held.

"We don't have much time," I said. "I want you to tell me everything that happened after you and David parted ways."

The look on his face told me Badger was frightened. As he spoke, the mask of indifference and anger fell away.

I listened without interruption to his account until he'd finished.

"That's what happened," he said.

An officer approached. It was time to leave.

"Badger," I said, "If you've told me the truth…"

"I have!"

"Good. At least I know who to talk to next."

The officer motioned for me to leave.

I gave a smile of support to Badger. "Keep the faith."

Faith would be the only thing to save this man.

Rainbow was waiting for me by the front desk.

I took Teddy from her.

He shook, happy to see me again.

"Let's go. We have no time to waste."

As Rainbow drove she didn't say a word.

The silence was killing me.

I had to break it.

"He's scared," I said.

"I know. He should be. What an absurd thing to do! I'm sorry, Jillian. I want you to know how grateful I am for your trying to help."

"No need to apologize. You've been through a terrible ordeal, and now it's been compounded."

"Did you learn anything that might help him?"

"Perhaps. It's imperative I talk to Leo Hunter before this goes too far."

"Leo Hunter? He was staying at the Empress."

"Kelly will know how to reach him."

A look of consternation passed over her face.

"Kelly Morrison the administrative assistant?"

"Yes. Do you know her well?"

I was treading on thin ice.

"Not well. She worked closely with David. Sometimes he mentioned her. They went rock climbing together once."

Rainbow fell into silence.

No matter. We'd reached the hotel.

"I'll be praying for Badger. Don't give up!" I said.

A faint smile crossed her lips. She gave a slight nod then drove away.

It was strange. Rainbow was grieving, I understood, but her mind seemed to be preoccupied with something important.

Father Goodman and Rainbow held back, but why?

Maybe I didn't have their full trust.

I would have to prove myself.

It had been a tense day so far. I needed rest and food!

"Teddy, let's see if Arthur and Diana will join us for a late lunch...or afternoon tea!"

He wagged his tail at the two favorite meal words.

It made me smile as I sent my friends a text:

Any chance of afternoon tea? I need to make one call and I'll be free.

Diana responded a few seconds later:

Perfect. Arthur's free to watch Teddy. Let us know when you've made your call.

After reaching the room I kicked off my shoes and found a comfortable spot to call Kelly.

When she answered I hardly recognized her voice.

"Hi, Jillian."

"Hello, Kelly. You sound ill. Are you feeling okay?"

"Not really. I'm still a little depressed."

"I'm sorry. You'll need some time before feeling normal again. Remember that."

"I know. How can I help you?"

"How can I get a hold of Leo Hunter? It's important that I talk to him immediately."

"Leo? He's still here at the hotel. I'm with him now. We're wrapping up few things. I can set up an appointment, if you want."

"That would be wonderful. The sooner the better. A text will be fine."

"Where do you want to meet?"

"Let's say Palm Court. It would be better to meet on equal footing."

"The one with the stained glass dome?"

"That's the one. Thanks, Kelly."

"No problem. I'll do it now."

The appointment was set for 5 pm. I would probably be his last one for the day.

Lowest person on the totem pole.

To Leo Hunter, I was probably an insignificant nobody compared to the important government officials he worked with.

I wondered what really went on between him and David regarding the fishing business poised to encroach on the First Nations protected salmon runs.

My stomach growled. I sent a text to Diana to let her know I was ready.

"Time for tea, Teddy. Except you'll be with Arthur. I'll bring you a tidbit, I promise."

Teddy panted.

I hugged him close, attached his leash, and walked him to my friend's room.

"Here's the baby." I handed Arthur the leash. "Thanks for watching him for me."

Arthur scooped up Teddy, detached the leash, and held him close.

"You ladies enjoy your tea. We guys will watch TV and kick back."

"Come on, Jillian. You must be famished. It's almost three o'clock." Diana planted a goodbye kiss on Arthur's cheek.

Afternoon Tea at the Fairmont Empress was quite an experience. Diana and I were treated as if we were royalty from the moment we arrived in the Tea Lobby.

A pianist played a classical selection which soothed my spirit.

I put aside what I was about to ask Leo Hunter and concentrated on fully enjoying our experience.

A host seated us.

"This way, ladies."

We followed him to a table by the black marble fireplace ablaze with a warm fire for ambiance.

"Perfect." Diana said.

The china was an elegant Royal Doulton pattern of the Empress's signature tableware used since 1939. On the inside of each cup was a jeweled British crown affixed with a cross.

Simply lovely!

"Well, Jillian," Diane said, "We finally made it."

"Even Harrods in London wasn't this fancy, I'll have to admit."

A slight memory of a happier time flickered, but only for a moment.

"Here's your tea, ladies." After asking for milk or sugars, the server poured out.

A tiered stand held wonderful treats of delicious finger sandwiches, scones, tarts, and truffles. Many were made on site.

"You *were* hungry, Jillian." Diana nodded to the empty plates.

"I didn't eat everything. I did save a few bites for Teddy. At least we won't need dinner," I said."

"Oh, but Arthur will."

We chuckled.

It was good to laugh after being in a jail cell with Badger Knight.

"I'm going to need a nap after all this." I sipped the last drop of tea and placed my napkin on the table.

"Me, too." After signing the tab, she stood to leave.

"Thank you for this lovely treat, Diana. I was going to pay but wasn't fast enough."

"You're welcome. There's a lot on your mind. You can get the next one."

We smiled at our agreement.

The music gradually faded as we made our way back to the room. I hated for the pleasantness to end.

Teddy enjoyed the morsels I'd saved for him of finger sandwich and cake.

"You're spoiled rotten!" I teased.

"Woof!" he barked back.

"Let's have a nap before our meeting with Leo. Come on up to the bed, little one."

I scooped him up and laid him beside me, stroking his fur.

"Funny," I said to no one in particular. "I was saving Leo for last, and now I know why."

CHAPTER THIRTEEN

Leo Hunter changed our meeting to be held in his room at the Empress, which was actually a palatial suite. A sly move to allow him a position of power, I thought.

A pale blue entry, furnished with exquisite contemporary furnishings, led to an elegant living room with views overlooking the city.

Kelly showed the way to Leo's private inner sanctum where he sat behind a desk cluttered with paperwork.

A closer inspection of the man revealed tell-tale signs of ill health. His skin was blotchy, his breathing labored, and he was quite heavy.

In spite of obvious air conditioning, Leo Hunter perspired probably from being overweight, or maybe he was anxious about something.

"Mrs. Bradley to see you." Kelly stepped away.

He appeared surprised.

"Ah. The lady with the pooch. I've seen you two around the hotel. I believe we met at the conference."

"How kind of you to remember. I hope you don't mind Teddy coming along. Leaving him alone in a hotel room has proven disastrous in the past."

"Not at all." He motioned to a side chair. "Please have a seat and tell me what this is all about."

I placed Teddy near me on the floor and sat in the armless leather chair.

"Teddy, stay."

He obeyed.

"Good dog." I whispered. "I've come directly from the police station."

He stiffened.

"Was there a robbery?"

The man was cunning.

"No. Badger Knight has been arrested."

He looked stunned.

"Badger? What has he done now?"

"The police think he killed David Blackwolf."

Leo shrugged. "I suppose I could see that happening. They were always at odds."

"I believe he's innocent."

"Okay. That makes one person on his side. Now what has all this to do with me?"

Kelly opened the door slightly. "Do you need anything else this afternoon?"

"Wait for me, Kelly. This won't take long."

She closed the door.

Leo rose, stuffed a few papers into a folder, and took his coat from the back of his chair.

"State your case, ma'am. I'm a busy man and don't have time to have a discussion about a hot headed aboriginal killing one of his own people."

"Badger told me you and David had a heated discussion the night David was killed."

"So what? I told the police I'd talked to him."

"Yes. Early in the evening, you said."

"Wait a minute. Why are you going around sticking your nose into this? You sound as if you're part of the investigation."

"Perhaps I am. And you'd better tell me what went on that night because Badger saw you leave David's room and not when you told the police."

Leo Hunter sat back down.

"What do you want?"

"The truth."

He sighed.

"This is off the record and I'll deny anything I'm telling you if it ever goes to court, understand?"

"Perfectly. Now tell me what happened when you went to see David."

Leo looked nervous. He stood and paced, hands tucked inside his pants pockets.

"David found a loophole for a certain fishery to occupy lands previously dedicated to First Nations."

"So what was the problem? I thought you and your people wanted the fishery to get the contract."

"We did. Until I found out they promised David an exorbitant amount of money if he overlooked their illegal business practices."

"Do you believe he would have gone along with them?"

Teddy popped up his head.

"That's what we argued about. David knew this fishery would get its way eventually. Some crooked politician would go along. It happens."

This from a man wearing an expensive suit, monogrammed cuffs on his starched white shirt, and expensive looking diamond rings on his hands.

"You exclude yourself, of course."

He threw a cold look.

"I'll ignore your comment."

"I apologize."

"David proposed doing what they wanted and using the money to help his people."

"Noble of him."

"And stupid. I liked David. He was a good lawyer, and I'm sorry someone killed him."

He paused.

"You want the truth?"

I nodded.

"When I left David's room he was alive. If Badger

Knight claims he saw me leave it will be his word against mine."

"I believe I've heard enough." I scooped up Teddy and held him close. "Thanks for your time."

"Kelly will show you out."

I turned.

"I can find the door." With a pointed perusal of the suite, I left Leo standing by his desk, red-faced and frowning.

On the way out, Kelly whispered. "I'll call you."

I simply nodded.

The interview left me tired and at loose ends. I was no closer to discovering the truth.

Lord, please show me the way.

"Come on, Teddy. We need dinner."

"Woof!" he barked as if to say, "Indeed we do, Mistress."

The restaurants at the hotel had excellent food. The one that caught my attention, however, was the curry buffet in the Bengal Bar.

Indian food was one of my favorites, following Mexican, and Italian.

It was still early evening. I texted Arthur and Diana to learn their dinner plans before I'd be able to make mine with Teddy along.

After a few moments, she texted back:

Staying in this evening. Will watch Teddy for you – no problem.

Perfect.

Teddy enjoyed a slice of duck breast I'd saved and rinsed off from the previous night. I didn't think he'd care for the sauce.

"Fresh water is all you need now." I rinsed his bowl and poured in some bottled water left over from the Gold Lounge. "Only the best for my sweet little friend."

He lapped thirstily after eating the leftovers while I dressed for dinner.

I selected a blue dress with a necklace of black crystals and pearls. It was one of my favorite outfits.

It would be lonely to eat by myself, but I needed time to reflect on the case.

"Let's get your leash on, Teddy, and go see Arthur and Diana. What do you say, boy?"

"Woof! Woof!"

"They don't spoil you or anything, do they?"

He wagged his tail as if he understood perfectly.

Teddy pranced ahead until we reached their room.

"Come in, come in." Diana made a sweeping gesture toward Arthur clutching a bright blue ball.

"Found it in a specialty shop yesterday and I couldn't resist."

Teddy saw it immediately and pawed Arthur's leg to play fetch.

"At least I won't be missed," I said.

With Teddy settled with Arthur I made my way to the Bengal Lounge.

An authentic tiger skin from the days of the Empire hung above the massive fire place. The room as well as the entire hotel drew inspiration from Queen Victoria's role as the Empress of India.

Delicious aromas from the buffet wafted my way as a host offered to let me sit anywhere I wished.

A leather winged back chair near a window offered privacy with a view of the entire lounge.

"This will do nicely," I said to the server. "I'll have water with a slice of lemon, cranberry juice, and do the buffet."

"Thank you. I'll get your drinks."

Tiny portions of Chicken Tandoori roasted in a clay pot, butter chicken – succulent pieces of chicken breast simmering in a tomato cream sauce, basmati rice, chicken curry, lentils with tomatoes, and samosas – one of my favorite croquettes stuffed with potatoes, filled my plate.

I ladled creamy raita – a spicy yogurt based condiment with cucumber and red onion over everything, filled a small bowl with more, and returned to my table overlooking the city.

The server placed a basket of warm naan on the table to enjoy with my meal.

I would dip the flatbread into the raita for a wonderful tasty treat.

As I ate my dinner I relaxed in this magnificent paneled room with coffered ceilings, fan palms, and polished wood floors.

The server was attentive without being intrusive. She refilled my water and kept an eye on me in case I needed anything.

With wonderful service and the added ambiance of live jazz filling the room with smoky bar-room classics, I felt happy.

A clink of glasses across the room interrupted my mood.

Seated at a corner table was Leo Hunter and a man I'd never seen before.

As suspicious as always, I pretended to take a selfie. Instead, I aimed the camera at Leo and his table mate and clicked.

Kelly would probably know who the man was. She'd promised to call me.

I had an uneasy feeling about Leo Hunter. Maybe he was telling the truth about David cutting a deal with the fishery.

Or maybe Leo was the one cutting the deal.

At any rate, David couldn't defend himself.

Leo had the upper hand. For now.

If Badger Knight could pinpoint the time he saw Leo leave David's room, it might put Leo at the scene at the time of the murder.

Stone would be able to find out. I'd call him first thing in the morning.

Coffee sounded good for dessert. With a simple smile

directed her way, the server came to my table.

"Would you please bring me a cappuccino? Three sugars, please."

Coffee for dessert made me feel decadent. I'd drink it every night if someone made it for me.

The steaming cup of frothy cappuccino came with biscotti.

A perfect ending to the meal.

Leo Hunter and his companion rose to leave.

I turned toward the window to avoid being seen.

He probably wouldn't recognize me without Teddy.

This was one time I was glad he didn't come.

As I signed the check a notification popped up on my phone.

It was from Kelly.

I'm at the hotel. Are you free to chat a few minutes? Kelly

How opportune.

Meet me in the Gold Lounge in five minutes. Jillian

The lounge was quiet and fortunately unoccupied. Plus, I could have an uninterrupted talk without Teddy to distract with his cuteness.

Kelly arrived looking tired.

"Have you been working all this time?" I asked, amazed at the way she was being taken advantage of.

"Pretty much." She plopped down in an overstuffed chair.

"Can I get you something to drink?"

"A cup of tea would be nice. Thank you, Jillian. My feet are killing me."

"Take off your shoes."

"I think I will." She slipped off her pumps and sat back.

"Thanks for meeting me. I couldn't help overhearing what Leo was telling you."

"You probably know everything anyway. I wouldn't worry."

She smiled.

"You need to know that David wasn't the one to uncover the shady business practices of that fishery."

"Leo Hunter?"

She nodded. "And you never heard that from me."

"Fair enough. Are you saying Leo was trying to keep what he'd found out from David?"

"And cinch the deal?"

"I see. Kelly, I have a photo of Leo and a man he had dinner with tonight."

I brought it up on my phone.

"Take a look and tell me if you recognize him."

She took my phone and studied the photo.

"That's him. I won't tell you his name because I would hate for it to come back to me."

"I understand. Is he the man representing the fishery in question?"

She nodded.

"Okay. And I didn't hear it from you."

Kelly smiled.

It was time to go get Teddy.

CHAPTER FOURTEEN

Teddy welcomed his special spot on the bed.

"Arthur must have worn you out with that..." I hesitated to say the word.

Thankful that Arthur had taken Teddy for his nightly walk, I got ready for bed.

Since I wasn't sleepy I reached for a notepad and pen next to my bed and jotted down a few facts about the case.

Raymond Crow went to see David around seven or seven-thirty (he says) to talk David out of helping the fishery take over the First Nations fishing site. Raymond said he left before eight.

Kelly Morrison met with David earlier in the evening regarding business around seven (she says). Did she see Raymond Crow who says he was there about the same time? Did he see her?

David was bludgeoned and stabbed in the heart with the talking stick shortly before eleven.

Rainbow met with David that night about nine-thirty (she says).

Rainbow says David told someone to come back later. Who?

Rainbow and David ate or drank nothing. Why were two glasses on the counter when he was killed?

Badger Knight and Leo Hunter went to David's room that night. What time?

Thinking about the details of the case made me tired.

Tomorrow I would take another look and add Sergeant Stone's information to the mix.

We were drawing closer. But to whom?

When I tried to reach Stone the next morning he didn't respond. I left a message for him to call me.

There wasn't much more I could do without the timeframe of Badger's testimony.

Maybe it was a good time to visit the Butchart Gardens. It would clear my head to immerse myself in beauty for a change.

Arthur had previously mentioned plans for whale watching with Diana today.

As amazing as it would be to see a whale pop out of the water, I would rather visit gorgeous gardens any day.

Dressed in stretch jeans, a cute blue and yellow print top, and wearing comfortable shoes, I fed Teddy, then went to the Gold Lounge.

Two cups of coffee and a croissant later, I was ready to embark on what I'd come for.

Downstairs, the concierge handed me a colorful trifold brochure.

"The Butchart Gardens are one of our most popular destinations. Enjoy the tour, Ms. Bradley. May I call a cab for you?"

"Yes, thank you."

Moments later, Teddy and I were on our way.

The weather was balmy, the landscape verdant, and Teddy and I had our tummies full.

He sat happily on my lap, panting now and then to release any stress about going to a place he'd never been.

From the documentary I remembered the Butchart family originally mined limestone from the quarry for their Portland Cement Company.

When the stone was exhausted, Mrs. Butchart created the sunken gardens to replace the quarry.

"Here we are, ma'am." The driver nodded to the large yellow sign at the entrance.

After paying him, he dropped us off in the parking lot where we could walk in.

I put on my straw hat to protect my fair skin from the sun, placed Teddy in his carrier for safe keeping, and found the ticket booth.

Having checked online beforehand I knew I wanted a leisurely self-guided walking tour punctuated with lunch and afternoon tea.

Teddy could walk part of the distance, but I'd carry him when he tired.

If there could be a ninth wonder of the world I would suggest this 50 acre garden paradise. The brochure states close to a million visitors come here annually.

For good reasons. The Sunken Garden, where it all began, with its serene lake and magnificent fountain soaring 70 feet into the air, was phenomenal. And the Rose Garden, with its rose laden arches in summer and bronze Italian cast Sturgeon Fountain, was another sterling example.

Children would love the park, too, with its charming carousel and ice cream stands.

Totem poles stood at one point. The carved faces reminded me of Raymond Crow making a shame pole for David Blackwolf.

The victim had at least one obvious person against him.

Once inside, I took Teddy out and attached his leash.

As we walked through the epic Sunken Garden, drinking in the beauty of azaleas, rhododendrons, and tulips, he sniffed the ground and wagged his tail in delight at the new smells he found.

At one point Teddy found delight in chasing a nearby peacock.

I was happy to find doggie waste bags and water stations conveniently located.

We strolled through the Japanese Gardens with stunning arrays of Himalayan blue poppies until I needed to rest.

"Let's get some lunch in the dining room, what do you say, Teddy?"

It was too late. I had said the word "lunch."

"Woof! Woof!" he barked, causing heads to turn.

A little uneasy about taking Teddy into the dining room in case he should bark again, I put him back in his tote, and approached the desk.

"Lunch for one," I told the host busy with her reservation list.

"Name?" she asked.

"Jillian Bradley."

The rather plump host looked up with a wide smile.

"*The* Jillian Bradley of the 'Ask Jillian Column?'"

"That's me."

She jiggled. "Oh my. This is so exciting! Excuse me for just a moment. Wait here. I'd like to let the manager know you're here."

She motioned for another woman to man the desk, then crossed the room.

I stepped aside for the next in line and waited, watching where the host went.

She found a man sporting a gray goatee and mustache who appeared to be engaged with a server.

Nodding my way, the host said a few words to her manager who immediately left his present concern and headed toward me.

"Mrs. Bradley, this is an honor!" the manager said. After introductions, he gathered a menu and took a brief look at Teddy.

"Won't you please come this way?"

A few guests gawked and pointed as we passed their tables.

"I'll seat you on the patio at our special table overlooking the gardens. We usually don't allow dogs inside, but we're happy to make an exception for a celebrity."

"Thank you. That's very kind."

Problem solved.

The lunch was lovely. Light with a Cobb salad and steamed lemon pudding for dessert.

I looked down at Teddy nestled in his carrier on the floor beside me.

"Ready to tackle another garden?"

Teddy perked up his ears.

"Okay, let's go."

We strolled through the amazing Italian Garden with its Star Pond and bronze statue of Mercury.

Before visiting the last garden I had to have afternoon tea, which was superb.

The Mediterranean Garden, with its array of drought resistant plants from various parts of the world that had similar growing conditions, was the last area to visit.

The tour had been amazing.

I couldn't wait to write an article for my column.

Our taxi arrived soon and took us back to the hotel.

Teddy and I were exhausted, but in a good way.

I gave him fresh water before we lay down for a brief nap.

As my head hit the pillow, Sergeant Stone finally answered my call.

"Jillian? Stone here. What's going on?"

"Thanks for answering back. I never did get what time Badger Knight said he went to see David Blackwolf."?"

"I have it in my notes. Do you think it's important?"

"It could be. Leo Hunter wasn't forthcoming about the

time. In fact, he is a huge suspect in my mind. We'll talk."

"Here it is. Ten-fifteen."

"Ten-fifteen. And Rainbow says she was with David at nine-thirty, which wasn't long for a visit if you ask me."

"No. I agree. This isn't like the plot in 'Murder on the Orient Express' where everyone was the murderer?"

"I don't believe it is. But the times are unusually close! If everyone is telling the truth, it would mean David had an hour and a half unaccounted for."

"I'll check room service at the Empress and see if anything was delivered."

"Good. He may have gone out."

"Perhaps. Or maybe he took a shower and got ready for Rainbow's visit."

"That seems more plausible."

"She told me David had appointments and files to work on before he could see her."

"So you think he saw Kelly and Raymond Crow around seven."

"Yeah. Then he may have worked on the files a while before cleaning up."

"No use to speculate, Jillian. I'll contact the hotel and find out about room service and get back to you."

"Okay. After my visit to the Butchart Gardens today I'll be taking ibuprofen and going to bed early. If I don't respond right away you'll understand."

"I will. And Jillian – thanks for your help. You're top stuff."

"Thank you, Sergeant. We'll find him."

"Or her."

CHAPTER FIFTEEN

By the next morning, strolling through the Butchart Gardens had taken their toll on my lower back and legs. I suppose climbing the stairs out of the Sunken Garden was the culprit.

"Oh, Teddy. I'm sore!"

He cocked his head at my complaint.

"What can I do to help?" he seemed to ask.

"A hug will do nicely."

He pranced to me and licked my cheek.

I gathered him close and kissed him on top of his head.

"I do love you, you know."

"Woof!" he barked as if to say, "I love you, too – especially when you feed me."

"You're right. It's time for breakfast."

Once again, I was happy I had laid out an outfit the night before. I slipped on a long white skirt, black tank top, and jean jacket.

A pair of gold sandals and a black and white pendant completed my ensemble for the day.

"Coffee first, dear doggie, then I'll make something for you."

With Teddy slung over my shoulder in his tote, I made my way to the Gold Lounge, poured a cup of coffee to go, and returned to the room.

I took him out and set him on the floor. He marched over to his small basket of toys and selected a rather worn blue stuffed pig.

"You want to play, don't you? Okay." I tugged the eyeless pig away and threw it across the room. "Fetch!"

He perked up his ears, raced to retrieve his plaything, and carried it back with a death grip in his mouth.

"That's enough for now. After I feed you we'll take a walk. Maybe we'll see something interesting."

Teddy sat nearby and watched intently as I prepared his meal of meat scraps, small chunks of apple, and a few bits of whole grain bread.

"Some fresh water and you'll be ready for the day, little one."

In a few seconds Teddy ate everything on his plate, licking it clean.

"My goodness, you were hungry! Now it's time for mine."

With Teddy leashed and inside his little carrier, I returned to the Gold Lounge and had a leisurely brunch of pastries, fruit, and freshly squeezed orange juice.

"We'll go back to the room so I can freshen up before we go exploring."

Another guest sitting nearby eyed me with a raised brow when I spoke to Teddy.

I smiled at the woman.

"Have a good day," I said as I left.

Back in the room I took some pain reliever, and got Teddy ready with his paraphernalia.

Before we left, I went to the window to see what kind of a day it was.

I lifted the sash.

The harbor beckoned with sea air and cries of gulls.

"Let's go to Fisherman's Wharf."

Teddy popped up his head and perked up his ears as if to say, "A fine idea, Mistress!"

With hotel key and wallet safely tucked inside a pocket on Teddy's tote we left the room.

Down the hall on the way to the elevator, housekeepers were busy cleaning rooms and wishing guests good morning.

A lovely hotel. Too bad it was tainted with murder.

David Blackwolf was not the first victim at the Empress. I'd read the history before I left home of more than one ghost on the premises.

One of the reported specters was the hotel's architect Francis Rattenbury. Another was a former maid seen on the 6th floor. The apparition of a construction worker who hanged himself has also been seen.

Would David Blackwolf join their ranks, I wondered.

By the time I came out of my contemplation, Teddy and I had walked to the harbor. We were exploring colorful houseboats moored on either side of a dock when a familiar voice called out.

"Ahoy!"

It was Gerald poking out from a dilapidated houseboat, desperately in need of renovation.

"Ahoy, yourself!" I said.

Teddy was happy to see his new friend.

Gerald put down his hammer and bent to pick him up.

"Good morning, boy. Out for a walk?"

"We are. I couldn't resist talking him for a walk around this delightful marina. I do love the sea."

"Me, too. Do you want to come aboard my boat?"

"I'd love to."

"Careful now." Gerald held my hand as I stepped on board of the small vessel.

"So you're going to create a sea-worthy home from this old dinghy?"

"Doing my best. I plan to build up. A two story for when I need to expand."

"I see."

"Want to see inside?"

He led the way with Teddy as I followed.

The inside reminded me of a mobile home I'd visited once. Compact, functional, and quite cozy.

"This is actually not too bad, Gerald. You have a sitting area, a kitchen, a bathroom, and looks as if you have a bedroom in back."

"Glad you approve. The inside is almost finished. Once I get it painted and a few pots of shrubs on the patio it will make me happier."

"Has Rainbow seen it?"

He put Teddy on the floor, and wiped his brow with a rag.

"I showed it to her when I first bought it. Haven't had the nerve to ask her over again. It would be better to wait until it's close to being finished before I do."

"Sometimes women don't need a man to have everything perfect before they'll accept him."

Gerald looked at the floor.

"Do you really think I have a chance with her? I mean, with everything she's been through with David and all."

"It may take some time. If it's meant to be it will happen. If not, you move on."

He nodded. "I hope I won't have to."

"Tell me about your tour guide job with the ghost walk."

"The reason I took the position was I love the history of the island and could work at night."

"I'm dying to ask you – Have you actually seen a ghost?"

He smiled.

"Once, I think."

Teddy grew restless and panted.

"Oh, dear. I think we need to be going. Teddy needs to finish his walk and take his morning nap."

"Tough life."

We chuckled.

"Thanks for the tour. I'll have to see it when you add the second floor."

"You're welcome anytime, Jillian. Let me know when you want to take the ghost tour."

"I will. And sometime you'll have to tell me about the one you saw."

We waved goodbye.

Gerald ducked back inside.

As I left, I could hear hammering.

Sergeant Stone sent a text:

Wanted to let you know Badger Knight freed on a technicality. Somehow he never signed the confession. Not enough physical evidence to hold him, anyway.

I answered:

What can I say? He is a lawyer. Any word on David Blackwolf's activity from eight to nine-thirty?

Stone replied:

There was a record of room service delivering a meal for one. Looks as if he was alone.

Teddy and I had reached Government Street along the harbor. Waiting for Teddy to catch his breath a moment, I studied the old hotel built over a hundred years ago in 1908.

It almost looked spooky. Especially after Gerald's and my discussion of ghosts. With unlocked windows, I wondered if anyone had fallen to their death.

Teddy tugged on his leash letting me know he was ready to walk again.

I snapped out of my chain of thoughts. A hidden piece of information about who killed David Blackwolf niggled in my brain.

This hotel held secrets.

It was up to me to unlock the secret of who killed David Blackwolf. If only I had enough clues!

"Teddy, I want you to be on the alert for any clues that will help us identify the killer."

"Woof! Woof!" he barked.

"I do believe you understand. Good."

If only I could talk to Badger Knight again. I felt sure he could bring light to the mystery.

It was time to give Father Goodman a call.

"Jillian, it's nice to hear from you."

"I hope it's a good time to chat. You don't have a class or anything?"

"No, it's fine. My class isn't until this afternoon. How can I help?"

"Have you heard Badger's been released?"

Silence.

"Released, you say? No I hadn't heard. Rainbow hasn't come in yet. What do you want me to do?"

"Would you ask her to call me? It's important I talk to Badger again, and I don't know how to reach him."

"Certainly. No problem. She'll be in soon. Have you done any sightseeing at all with our police taking so much of your time?"

"Getting there. We went to the Butchart Gardens yesterday."

"We?"

"Teddy and me. He's quite a companion since I'm alone."

"I understand. Have you seen the Butterfly Gardens or visited the Royal British Columbia Museum?"

"Hopefully there'll be a chance to see them before I leave. Tell me, have you ever taken a ghost tour?"

He chuckled.

"You've been talking to Gerald, right?"

"Uh-huh. He says he thinks he's seen a real one."

"People do see things. I've wondered if the apparitions have to do with light waves. Scientists have captured sounds, so why not images?"

"You have a good point. Anyway I want to take a tour one of these nights."

"Why don't I join you?"

I was surprised a priest would offer to go with me.

"That would be wonderful. When are you free?"

He laughed.

"I'm free *every* night."

"I'm not much of a night person. Maybe a nap this afternoon will help keep me awake."

"Tonight then? I'll get the details and we'll make plans. Funny, I've always wanted to go on one of these but never found the right person to go with."

"I'll ask Arthur and Diana to watch Teddy. He might bark and ruin any special effects."

"It sounds as if you're a doubter to begin with."

"Perhaps. Angels – I believe in totally. Ghosts? A small maybe. Remind me to tell you about one I *think* I encountered in Half Moon Bay."

"I'll look forward to it."

CHAPTER SIXTEEN

Father Goodman was true to his word about setting up the details. He even went one step further and managed to book a walking tour with Gerald Dawson.

I stroked Teddy's fur.

"Teddy, I have some good news and some bad news."

He looked into my eyes and stretched back his ears, a sign of trepidation not knowing what to expect.

"The bad news is you can't go with me on the ghost tour tonight. But the good news is I'm going to ask Arthur and Diana to watch you."

At the mention of Arthur's name Teddy perked up his ears. All signs of misgivings disappeared.

As if on the same wave length, Diana sent a text:

If you're free how about dinner tonight?

A perfect entree. I texted back:

I can meet you anytime!

She answered:

Let's say seven. Arthur will find a dog-friendly restaurant.

I loved these people. I typed back:

Thanks. I'll come to your room. See you soon!

After reading up on the ghost tours and discovering the walk could be at least two miles, I needed to prepare.

"Let's lie down, sweet doggie." I scooped him up, set him on the bed, and kicked off my shoes.

My phone alarm was set to give us at least an hour to

nap before dressing for dinner.

I lay down on the cloud soft pillows, pulled the fluffy comforter over me, and closed my eyes.

Lord, please renew my body with this rest. I'll need strength for tonight.

All worry and care immediately left and I fell asleep.

Before long, the alarm buzzed and woke me.

I tapped it off, stretched, and got up.

Teddy popped up his head and stretched awake, then shook himself, fluffing out his fur.

"Time for me to get dressed for dinner and make your supper before we go.

"Come on little guy." I gathered him in my arms, kissed his head, and set him on the floor."

"What shall I wear that will look dressy but will be comfortable for a walking tour?"

"Ah, my long African print skirt, black tee, and jean jacket will be perfect."

"Woof!" barked Teddy.

I chuckled

"So you approve?"

"Woof!" he barked again.

"Oh, I think that means you want your dinner."

He wagged his tail at the correct answer.

"You're some dog, Teddy. I hope you can prove again how special you are by helping me with this case. It's still cloudy."

This time he growled softly.

"You agree?"

Uncanny the way he understood everything I said.

I set his bowl of meat scraps, peas, carrots, and whole grains on the floor.

"Dig in!"

In a flash the dish was licked clean.

With a quick brush of my hair, some lipstick, and a spritz of perfume I was ready.

My brain recalled a few times I'd dressed for dinner dates, with butterflies of anticipation.

No butterflies this time. They'd all flown away by this stage of my life.

I shook myself free of past memories and focused on Teddy instead.

"Time to put on your leash and get out your carrier. We're going to see Arthur and Diana."

Teddy panted with anticipation, probably for a chance to play ball with his friend.

At seven o'clock sharp I rapped on the Wingate's door.

Diana invited me in. "Jillian! Prompt as usual. Hello, Teddy." She patted his head, picked him up, and gave him a hug.

"Hi, Jillian." Arthur couldn't wait to take Teddy from Diana. "Hello, boy. Ready for an outing?"

Teddy licked his cheek.

Arthur laughed. "I guess that means yes."

"Where are we off to?" I asked.

"Café Brio." Arthur stroked Teddy. "I reserved a dog friendly table on their patio."

"Wonderful!" I thought now would be a good time to ask him to watch Teddy. "Arthur, I'm going on a ghost tour with Father Goodman after dinner and wondered if you would watch Teddy."

Diana eyed me. "A late night date with a priest?"

"Well, he offered and I really couldn't say no."

We laughed.

"Sure, Jillian. Teddy will be fine with me. What time do you think you'll get home?" Arthur asked.

I blushed.

"The tour starts at nine-thirty and lasts an hour and a half. Shall we say around eleven? I know that's rather late."

Diana intervened.

"It's not a problem. I'm usually still awake and can let you in. Please send me a text so I'll know it's you."

"Thanks. I will, especially since there still may be a murderer on the loose."

She shuddered.

"Do you really think it was a random killing?"

"No, I don't. Whoever killed David Blackwolf meant to end his life. The police and I still aren't sure why, but we're working on it."

Arthur opened the door. "They have the best amateur sleuth, and dog, working on it."

I smiled, reminiscing of the time I worked with Detective Noble in Scottsdale. Noble was the one who named Teddy "sleuth dog."

"Ready, ladies?" Arthur swept his hand through the door opening, and we headed downstairs.

Once we were in the lobby, Arthur turned to me.

"It's a four block walk. Would you rather take a cab since you'll be walking later?"

He was so thoughtful.

"I don't know about Jillian, but I'll need a ride," Diana said to him.

"I'm sorry, darling. You usually enjoy walking. I'll hail a cab."

Arthur sat in the front seat, with Diana, Teddy, and me in the back. The ride only took a few minutes. He paid the driver and helped us out of the cab.

"Right this way, ladies."

When we stepped from the cab I was immediately taken with Arthur's choice for the evening.

Café Brio was a café straight out of Italy with a Tuscan exterior. A vine covered arch led through a garden courtyard and into the restaurant.

"This is lovely, Arthur." Diana appeared pleased as well.

The host and servers treated us as if we were family, even welcoming Teddy with pats.

We were led to a tucked away table on the patio and handed menus. Our drinks arrived in a timely manner, including a small bowl of water for Teddy.

"Thank you," I said, impressed.

"They have interesting art work." Diana nodded to the walls.

"And they appear to be for sale." Fine art was one of my weaknesses, along with dessert.

"I wonder if I could fit one into my suitcase." I looked at Arthur.

"If it didn't, I'm sure we could arrange to have it shipped home."

"Good point, Arthur." I returned to the menu.

As much as I loved pasta, rarely turning down spaghetti and meatballs, I decided on the tempting rosemary salt marinated beef striploin.

"I don't think I can pass up fresh arugula, olive oil crushed potatoes, sautéed asparagus, and white wine and fresh tomato jus. Simply unavoidable!"

"Jillian," Diana whispered, "don't forget to check out the dessert menu, too."

She smiled conspiratorially at her husband.

"Oh, dear." My eyes widened at the choices. "How will I ever decide between the sticky date toffee pudding with the toffee-rum sauce and the pistachio and cocoa success cake with mocha gelato?"

Arthur and Diana smiled.

"At least we can order half orders of the entrees," I said. My conscious was assuaged.

The meal was delightful, and service impeccable. To top off the dinner, all of us ordered cappuccinos.

Teddy behaved well, only sniffing the food as it arrived at our table.

The server prepared a doggie bag for him without my having to ask.

"Now, tonight is my treat," I said when the check was presented. "You have been wonderful hosts and I want to thank you."

The dinner was worth every penny!

I reached on the floor and picked up my well-behaved little dog.

"Come along, Teddy. Into your tote."

On the way out I took one last look at the art. One in particular caught my attention. The small work captured the spirit of downtown Victoria with lovely hanging baskets and quaint shops. If this was meant to be mine, it would be here when I returned.

Arthur hailed a cab, which dropped me off at the Visitor Information Center where the tour was to begin.

"Thanks for watching Teddy for me." I patted my sweet puppy goodbye. "Be a good dog and don't wear Arthur out."

It was hard to leave Teddy with anyone. In the past, the first Teddy had been kidnapped when I left him alone in the hotel room.

Never again would I assume my dog was safe with anyone unless it was a trusted friend.

Father Goodman stood waiting on the curb. He helped me from the car.

After quick introductions to Arthur and Diana, we waved goodbye.

A small group had gathered in front of the Visitor's Center on this dark evening. I looked around for Gerald Dawson.

Father Goodman nodded. "There's Gerald in front of the woman with the backpack."

When the woman turned around, I was surprised.

Rainbow Knight had joined us.

CHAPTER SEVENTEEN

My mouth dropped open.

Rainbow half smiled. "Hello, Jillian. Father Goodman. You look surprised."

Gerald leaned in and whispered, "It was my idea to invite her." He stood back up. "Ladies and gentlemen, it's time to begin our walk."

Had Rainbow and Gerald been seeing each other? I turned to Father Goodman.

He shrugged as if to say, "I never mentioned the tour tonight."

The Empress Hotel was the first stop on our tour.

Gerald nodded toward the grand edifice. "Not only has the architect of this hotel Francis Rattenbury been sighted here, he's been sighted over at another one of his projects – the Parliament Buildings, as well.

"His body rests uneasily in an unmarked grave in Bournemouth, England, where he was savagely bludgeoned to death by his wife's lover.

"It's believed the apparition of the thin mustached man walking these halls with a cane is seeking recognition he craves, but does not receive, where he is buried."

Rainbow stayed close the entire evening. It was as if she wanted to keep an ear open to anything we might say.

As the tour continued, Rainbow dropped to the back.

Nudging Father Goodman, we did the same.

Out of earshot, Rainbow touched my arm.

"Jillian, I'm worried about Badger. He won't talk to me or anyone else."

"I wonder what's wrong."

"Something is bothering him. The last time I talked to him I suggested he talk to you."

"A neutral person in the situation, right?"

"Exactly. You need to know that we are Christians. The only thing is Badger seems far away now."

Father Goodman chimed in. "I told Rainbow you were a believer, Jillian."

In a way I was glad the subject came up. It might make things easier when I talked to Badger.

We caught up with the group and gave Gerald our full attention for the rest of the tour.

As we walked the streets, poking around where ghosts had been sighted, I thought Gerald made an excellent guide.

Before long, I found myself immersed in the history of early Victoria.

The city reminded me of Wild West days in America with gambling halls, brothels, and tales of murder.

From all the talk of ghosts, an eerie mood crept in. No one in the group was smiling, I noticed. A few couples held hands.

"And now, ladies and gentlemen," Gerald said pausing, "We've reached Bastion Square and Helmcken Alley, the most haunted part of Victoria."

Voices in the group murmured. A heightened sense of alertness rose as we searched in earnest for ghosts.

Rainbow smiled, catlike, and whispered, "Gerald knows how to play the crowd."

In spite of her comment I shivered.

Gerald shared the salient points.

"One of the reasons for the many sightings in Bastion Square is the Maritime Museum of British Columbia.

"The museum, located in the old Supreme Court

building, sits above the old site of the city's jail and first gallows."

One of the group spoke up. "Look!" He pointed at the wall behind Gerald.

A slight breeze chilled the air.

"What do you see?" Gerald whispered.

"It looks like a hanged man."

The crowd, including Father Goodman, Rainbow, and myself, searched where he pointed.

We saw nothing.

"You're not the first to sight a hanged man, sir." Gerald resumed his talk.

"Many of the men who were hanged still lie buried beneath its foundations."

The group buzzed as we moved on to the next site.

"How are you holding up?" Father Goodman asked.

"Okay so far. At least I'm able to rest on the benches once in a while.

"What about you?"

"I'm fine. I'm used to walking around the campus every day."

Shortly before eleven, the tour came to an end. Participants lined up to thank Gerald for the great job he did.

Father Goodman and I hung back until last, along with Rainbow.

After Gerald spoke to the last walker, he headed our way.

"Well? Did you have any sightings?" he asked.

All three of us shook our heads.

"At least one in the group did." Rainbow said.

Gerald said, "I have my car if anyone needs a lift home."

I wondered if that old saying, "Two's company, three's a crowd" applied in this situation.

"I have my car, thanks." Rainbow said.

Gerald's countenance fell but only for a moment.

"I'm glad you came. I'll see you later at work."

She nodded.

Before she slipped away I caught her arm.

"If you'll give me Badger's number and address I'll try to talk to him."

She took the backpack off, unzipped an outside pocket, and took out a piece of paper and a pen.

"That would be wonderful, Jillian." She wrote out the information I asked for and handed it to me.

"I'll start first thing in the morning."

"Goodnight, everyone. Thanks for a wonderful tour, Gerald."

He blushed.

"See you at work tomorrow, Rainbow."

Father Goodman and I waited while Gerald filled out a clipboard with the list of those on the tour and locked up the Visitor Center.

"I had fun tonight," I said. "Thanks for the invite."

"It was fun, in a creepy sort of way."

We chuckled.

He grew serious.

"I was surprised to find Rainbow with Gerald. And yet I honestly thought they'd do well together."

"Is that what's been bothering you all this time?" I asked.

"I'm an old softie when it comes to young love. Now listen, Jillian. Before you change the subject, you must promise to help me with my garden."

"I will. But it will have to be after I do everything I can to solve this case."

"Understandable. Any suspects?"

I took a deep breath.

"Unfortunately, I suspect everyone."

Father Goodman raised an eyebrow.

"Sorry to keep you waiting." Gerald gestured to the parking lot, then led us to his car.

"So, Gerald," Father Goodman said, "did that man really see the hanged man ghost or was he a prop?"

Gerald unlocked his car and opened the doors for us.

"I was as surprised as you were. Believe it or not, that was the first time anyone in one of my tours actually saw an apparition."

"So it must have been real." I thought about the question haunting me.

"Gerald, you said you thought you saw a ghost once. After what you just told us, I assume it wasn't on a tour."

After we climbed inside he started the engine.

"Tell you what. After I drop Father Goodman off I'll show you exactly where I saw it."

A shiver ran up my spine.

It was approaching midnight by the time we dropped Father Goodman off and came back to the harbor.

Gerald pulled into the parking lot of the Empress and got out of the car. "Come on, I'll show you where I saw the apparition."

"Okay, but only for a moment. I need to pick up Teddy."

We stood on one side of the hotel, looking up.

Gerald pointed to a set of windows on the fourth floor.

"Right there," he said.

"What exactly did you see?"

"It was dark, of course, but when I saw movement outside that window it stopped me in my tracks."

"What else?"

"The figure clutched the teeth of the dentil molding overhead and made its way along the outside wall."

I tried picturing it in my mind.

"Well, I thought I was seeing things." He laughed nervously.

"And then it disappeared?" I asked.

"Yeah. I guess I got distracted because I didn't see it anymore."

"How strange. Who knows? Maybe it was a ghost."

"Thanks for a wonderful tour, Gerald. Very impressive."

"Glad you enjoyed it. Give Teddy a pat for me."

"I will. Thanks for bringing me home. Goodnight."

"Night."

I texted Diana to let her know I was on my way. Getting home late was exhilarating. I was a teenager again, except for my feet.

After knocking softly on her door, Diana simply handed Teddy to me snuggly nestled in his carrier.

"Thank you!" I whispered.

She smiled and whispered. "No problem. Night."

Teddy tried wagging his tail but was too tired.

I lifted him out of his carrier and set him on the bed. He fell right asleep.

"That's what I want to do, too."

A bath would have to wait until morning. Besides, I wanted to be fresh and alert when I talked to Badger Knight.

Lord, please guide me tomorrow. Open Badger's heart. Amen.

The last thing I saw before falling asleep was my window with the sash closed. Tomorrow I would locate the room where Gerald saw his ghost.

CHAPTER EIGHTEEN

A low growl woke me. Teddy wagged his tail seeing I was awake. I checked the time.

Nine already?

"You poor doggie. I'll throw something on as fast as I can."

No need to mention the reason.

In spite of sore feet I actually felt full of vim and vigor this morning.

"Here we go," I said attaching his leash. "Now we're all set."

Teddy enjoyed his brief walk along the dog area perimeter.

A brown and white shih tzu tugged his owner toward us.

"He simply wants to play." The owner scooped up the friendly dog, tipped his brow, and walked away.

Teddy whined.

"I know, I know," I said. "You need playtime."

It's true. I hadn't given him any one-on-one for a while.

"But you played ball with Arthur last night, didn't you?"

"Woof!" he barked.

What a smart dog.

For a moment my conscious was eased.

"We'll play fetch after your food settles."

He wagged his tail, delighted.

After feeding Teddy and placing him in his tote, I meandered to the Gold Lounge for coffee and something to eat.

"Good morning, Jillian." Arthur and Diana sat at one of the tables near a window.

"Good morning." I put Teddy on the floor next to a nearby table.

"Stay." I looked at him firmly.

He poked his head down inside.

"Good dog."

With a plate of chocolate croissants and fresh pineapple chunks in one hand and a cup of coffee in the other, I took a seat.

Teddy poked his head up and sniffed the aroma of croissant.

I broke off a tiny piece without chocolate and gave him some.

"What are you guys up to today?"

Diana smiled at Arthur. "We decided to tour some gardens today."

Arthur sipped his coffee then set it on the table.

"Diana's business with the hotel has finished. They appreciated her glowing review. Now we have time for sightseeing."

"Lucky you." I took a sip of coffee. "The Butchart Gardens were fabulous."

"That's one of our destinations," Diana said. "The Butterfly Gardens are close by."

"Well, we'd better get going." Arthur stood and helped Diana out of her chair.

Seeing his loving gesture brought a brief twinge of sadness at my being alone.

I let it pass.

"Have a wonderful day. Will I see you for dinner?"

"We'll look forward to it. Why don't you choose a place tonight?"

"I will. Shall we say six?"

"Six it is." Diana patted my shoulder.

I pulled my phone from my purse and called Badger Knight.

Lord please let him answer and be willing to see me.

After three interminably long rings he answered.

"Badger Knight. How can I help you?"

"Badger, this is Jillian Bradley."

I waited for his response.

"Rainbow sent a text that you'd call. I've set aside some time to see you at my office this afternoon at two, if that's convenient."

"Works for me. Do you mind if I bring Teddy along? I've no one to watch him today."

"Sure. He's welcome."

"Thank you. If you'll give me your address I'll see you at two."

He complied.

Thank you Lord!

With four hours to kill I decided to take it easy for a change. Besides, I could rest up from last night.

I refilled my coffee and resisted eating another chocolate croissant. It would make keeping my weight down easier when I returned home. I probably gained a couple of pounds on this trip already.

"Come along, Teddy." I picked up his tote and returned to the room.

Once inside, Teddy wiggled out and raced to his toys.

I chuckled.

"You didn't forget my promise, did you?"

"Woof!" he barked.

"Okay. We'll play fetch. And while we're at it, let's review a few commands, what do you say?"

"Woof! Woof!" A double bark.

Things were going along quite nicely until noon, and I grew hungry again.

Then I remembered.

The windows!

I curled up in a chair and took my phone in hand.

"Let me search for a floorplan of this hotel. I'll bet I can find one."

After a few clicks on images I found what I was looking for.

I pinpointed approximately where Gerald had said he saw the apparition and made a note.

The next thing I would do would be to check with the lobby desk and find the room numbers.

Perhaps I would try a restaurant close to the hotel for lunch. On the way out I could get the information about the rooms.

What to wear to see Badger? Something understated, which would invite openness and trust.

I pulled out a pair of black slacks and selected a black camisole to wear under a dark blue blouse.

"Now for a necklace," I said.

A large silver link chain went perfectly with the outfit, adding the perfect touch of sophistication.

"Teddy," I said to him.

He perked up his ears.

"Should I wear low heels or flats? The heels do make me feel dressier."

Instead of a "woof" all I got from him was a yawn.

So much for Teddy's opinion on what I wore.

I had to chuckle. But I thought it was important for Badger to view me as a person to place his confidence in.

With two hours before I met with him, there was plenty of time to check out the windows and have lunch.

Before starting out I noticed Teddy's fur was unsightly.

"You need brushing, little one."

Setting him on the bathroom counter, I gave him a good brush out.

If Teddy were a cat he might have purred from the way he half closed his eyes as I stroked him.

"There. Now you're a real gentleman."

He panted as if to say, "I feel better, too."

With Teddy looking presentable I attached his leash, placed him in his carrier, and took one last look around the room.

I looked on the table. "Oh, dear. I can't forget my phone!"

Its ring startled me.

Sergeant Stone had called.

"Good day, Jillian. Just checking in. Thought you might be interested to hear that Leo Hunter is in the hospital.

"What happened to him?"

"It appears he had either a heart attack or a stroke."

Exactly as I feared.

"I'm sorry to hear that. Can he have visitors?"

"Not at the moment. Only immediate family since he's in intensive care. What's going on with you?"

"I have an appointment to talk with Badger Knight this afternoon."

"Badger? What does he want to talk to you about?"

"Rainbow asked me to talk to him. It's personal. He and I never had a real chance to talk in his cell."

"Yes, I know. Those are the rules."

"I'm hoping to clear up some questions I have about the night David Blackwolf was killed."

"I'll want to hear all about it after you've talked to him. Please call me, Jillian."

"I will if I think it's related to the case, of course."

There was a slight pause.

Before I gave him a chance to argue I ended the conversation.

"I must run. Lunchtime. We'll talk soon, Sergeant Stone. Please keep me informed on Leo Hunter."

"Why are you still interested in him?"

"Call it an instinct."

"Here we go."

"No, listen. Leo winding up in the hospital might have a

bearing on the fishing rights dispute."

"Good point. I'll call you if there's a change in his status."

"Thank you."

I hung up.

With Leo in the hospital and Badger out of jail things were certainly getting interesting.

The situation made me hungry.

CHAPTER NINETEEN

Since I was alone and had Teddy to consider, room service made sense for lunch.

As I read the menu I was reminded that David Blackwolf had ordered the night he was killed.

Had housekeeping also made their turn down service?

I would check with Sergeant Stone.

The hummus dip with a tomato and cucumber salad appealed. The light entrees would allow room for dessert.

Hmm.

It had been some time since I'd had cheesecake. This one sounded delicious – spiced graham crust, citrus wild berry compote, and sesame snap. Whatever a sesame snap was, I wanted one.

When the server arrived, I asked him about the turndown service.

"Daily housekeeping and the turn down service are offered upon request."

I vaguely remembered requesting them when I checked in.

"Thank you."

He set the tray on an ottoman and lifted the metal food covers.

"Is there anything else you require, ma'am?"

I signed the bill. "No, thank you. The food looks wonderful."

"You may call for housekeeping to retrieve your tray or

leave it outside your door."

"I will. Have a good day."

The server left.

Teddy waited patiently on the floor as I ate the lovely lunch. All I shared with him was a bite of carrot.

After lunch I retouched my lipstick, checked my hair for flyaways, and made sure I had my phone this time.

With Teddy in his tote strapped over my shoulder I stepped out of the elevator onto the first floor and walked to the lobby.

Guests were checking in and out at the front desk, but the line wasn't too long.

My turn came.

"May I help you, Ms. Bradley?" The cheerful clerk asked. Her name badge read Crystal Gable.

"Yes, Crystal. I need to locate the room numbers of this area of the hotel." I showed her the image on my phone.

"Of course." Crystal typed a few clicks on the computer. "Here we are."

She handed me the numbers on a slip of paper.

"This is exactly what I needed. Thank you, Crystal."

A sinking feeling came over me in the pit of my stomach.

Gerald had not seen an apparition.

He'd seen the killer.

We finally had a witness.

"Is there anything else I can help you with?" Crystal asked.

"Yes. Please call a cab. Thank you."

Crystal placed a call. "Your cab will arrive in five minutes."

"Thank you. We'll wait outside."

"I love your dog. He's well behaved!"

I smiled.

"Have a good day, Crystal and thanks again for your help."

"You too, Ms. Bradley. You too, Teddy."

He panted at the attention.

"Better let you on the grass before we head to Badger's office."

While we waited for the cab, I attached his leash and took him out. I let him roam a moment before the cab pulled to the curb, then placed him back inside.

"Where to, ma'am?" The driver asked opening the door for us.

I handed him the address from Badger I'd written down, climbed into the back seat, and set Teddy next to me.

"We'll be there in fifteen minutes." The driver squinted at me in his rear view mirror.

"You look familiar. Are you famous?"

I chuckled.

"Do you read garden columns?" I asked.

"As a matter of fact, I do. It's my hobby. Hey, now I recognize you. You write that 'Ask Jillian' column, don't you?"

"I do. It's nice to meet a reader."

He pulled into traffic. "Wow! Wait until I tell the wife. Can you sign something for me?"

"I'd be honored."

I noted his name on the license, found a card in my wallet, and pulled out a pen from my purse.

"To Hank, All the best, Jillian Bradley" I handed him the signature.

"Thanks a million, Ms. Bradley. You wrote an article once that saved my roses."

"Really? What was the problem?"

"I'd planted them where they retained too much water. I remember you said roses abhor getting their feet wet. What a picture!"

"Glad I was able to help."

Hank kept talking about his garden until we'd reached our destination.

I paid him and stepped out of the car.

"I'll see you in my column."

"You bet, Ms. Bradley. A real pleasure to meet you, ma'am."

There was that "ma'am" again. My wrinkles must be getting deeper. Perhaps it would enhance my level of respect when I talked to Badger.

"Well, here we are, Teddy." I held him.

He shivered. "There's nothing to worry about." I stroked his head. "We're here to help."

Teddy looked at me with his sweet brown eyes as if to say, "If you say so, Mistress."

I'd always thought difficult individuals were the result of difficult situations that had bested them.

Badger's office was located in a small strip center which included a couple of vacant storefronts.

Empty cups and fast food wrappers littered the parking lot. A huge black trash bag sat outside a hobby shop being vacated.

Lord, please go before me.

At least Badger's office was between two viable businesses.

After entering, I was pleasantly surprised to find a modest, but tidy, work space.

Badger stood behind his desk.

"Ms. Bradley, come in."

He shoved some papers inside a folder and closed the file. "Please, have a seat."

He motioned to a respectable brown vinyl chair that was not too uncomfortable.

"Thank you." I placed Teddy's carrier on the floor, then took him out.

Badger made no move to acknowledge him.

"May I get you some coffee? Tea?"

"No thank you. I'm fine."

He sat behind his desk.

"Tell me why you're here, exactly."

A typical question from a lawyer.

"Rainbow's concerned about you. I thought we could share some war stories."

He actually smiled.

"You, Jillian? War stories?"

"We all have them. Mine were being widowed early on, losing a second husband before we had any chance for happiness, and remaining childless."

He formed a tent with his hands.

"Definite war stories."

"I only have one."

I waited.

"When I was a small boy Rainbow, David, and I went to the river to play. I slipped down the hill, crashed into a pile of rocks, and wound up in the water."

"Go on." Even though I'd heard the story, it was important to get Badger's side.

"I must have hit my head on a rock because I went unconscious. When I woke up, my leg was in excruciating pain."

"You'd broken it?"

Badger nodded.

"David's father who was a doctor had set it while I was unconscious."

"I see."

"Do you?"

Badger seemed angry.

"The leg never set right. And before you ask, no, resetting it was not an option.""

"Why was that?"

"My father thought the limp would go away in time."

"But it didn't."

I wanted to say I was sorry, but sympathy was not what Badger needed to hear.

"Ever since then I've been a cripple. A cripple!" he

yelled.

I waited.

Teddy didn't move.

"And who is to blame for that?" I asked softly.

He slowly gave a reply.

"Can't you guess?"

I shuddered.

CHAPTER TWENTY

I sat still for a moment, shocked by the amount of anger in Badger's voice.

"Then you do blame someone." I shifted my position and gave Teddy a pat.

"Tell me, do you blame David Blackwolf for saving your life? Or his father for not setting your leg properly?"

Badger heaved a sigh.

"All these years I believe I blamed David's father. Looking back, though, I took it out on David."

I gave him a minute.

"Things changed between us after my leg healed and I was able to walk again. David excelled in school and in sports."

As he spoke, a shadow from the window crossed his face. It was as if he'd been living under David's shadow since the accident.

"Badger, haven't you ever heard the saying, 'It's not what happens to you, but your attitude toward what happens to you?'"

He shook his head.

"It's true." I leaned in. "You might have drowned that day. Then who would be looking after Rainbow? Or who would be an advocate for your people?"

The shadow passed. A look of understanding seem to replace it.

"You're a wise white woman," he said.

"Didn't you mean to say a wise *old* white woman?"

We chuckled.

The tension finally broke.

Teddy wiggled from my lap to the floor. He lay by my feet and put his head on his paws.

"Teddy's getting restless. We probably should go. But before we do, I need to ask you something."

"Of course. I've nothing to hide."

"That's good. We didn't have much time in that jail cell."

This time Badger shuddered.

"Tell me again exactly everything you did on the night David was killed. Don't leave out anything." I sat back.

He nodded.

"Okay. I worked late that night. Didn't leave the office until eight."

"Go on."

"I was hungry."

"Where did you eat?"

"At the first Burger King I could find."

I smiled. "Drive thru?"

He nodded again.

"That's good. Easy enough to find. There will be a record to verify your movement on their surveillance camera."

"I went home to eat my burger. After I ate I watched TV until I received a text from Rainbow."

"What time was this?"

"Must have been about nine. She said she wanted to talk."

"Did she say why?"

"No. But I guessed. I'd seen her with David at the meetings. I knew there was something between them."

"Did you talk with her?"

He shook his head, rose from his chair, and paced the room.

He shook his head.

"If I had, David might still be alive."

"So you didn't answer her text?"

"No. I had to have time to think. Jillian, David was a womanizer. I knew he wasn't good enough for Rainbow."

"Typical for an older brother to think. What did you do?"

"I went to see David and tell him to leave Rainbow alone."

"When was this?"

He looked at the ceiling.

"I'd just finished a program and about to start watching another one. I'd say about ten, as I told the police."

"And when you got to David's room what happened?"

"At first he wouldn't let me in. Then I saw Rainbow there. I got mad, forced my way in, and told her to leave. She kissed David. Kissed him right in front of me!"

"And how did you react?"

"I was too angry to talk to David rationally. I grabbed Rainbow by the elbow and escorted her out the door."

"This was at ten-fifteen?"

He sat back down at his desk.

"Yes. Right as we left, we bumped into Leo Hunter standing at the door."

"This is important, Badger. Try and remember anything unusual about Leo. His demeanor, his attire?"

Badger folded his hands.

"There was one thing. Leo carried a legal file. I recognized it right away."

"Good. That may be important."

Teddy stretched and yawned, then rose to his feet.

"Time to go outside, Mistress," he seemed to say.

I called a cab.

"We need to leave. Teddy needs to go outside."

Badger came from around his desk, as I attached Teddy's leash and gathered my purse.

"I'm going to pray that God will heal your heart, Badger."

"Thank you, Jillian. I could use a prayer dealing with Rainbow, too."

"I will. She'll be fine, in time."

He opened the door for us.

Teddy found a grassy area and sniffed around.

As the fresh air washed over me, something ticked in my brain.

When Badger originally gave his statement, he'd told the police he saw Leo Hunter *coming out* of David's room at ten-fifteen.

A minute ago, he told me Leo Hunter was *going into* David's room.

I needed to ask Rainbow and Leo again to get their stories straight on the timeframe.

Someone wasn't telling the truth.

Why?

Was Badger protecting Rainbow? Or Rainbow protecting Badger?

Perhaps Leo Hunter was trying to protect himself.

He would be if he was the last person to see David. At least the last *known* person to see him.

The cab arrived to take us back to the hotel.

Teddy and I climbed into the backseat and avoided eye contact with the driver.

I scooted Teddy into his tote to keep him calm so I could think.

If only I could talk to Leo Hunter. Maybe there was a way.

I texted Kelly:

How are you? I need your help in getting a message to Leo Hunter. Thanks! Jillian

Kelly was quick to respond:

I'm okay. Leo's in the hospital. He's had a bad heart attack. His family has been called in. I'm going over to the hospital right now.

I didn't divulge that Sergeant Stone had already told me.

I texted back:

I'm sorry to hear. Which hospital is he in?

After jotting down the necessary information, we arrived back at the Empress.

The cab pulled to the curb of the hotel entry.

I paid the fare, then turned to Teddy as we entered the lobby.

"We need to find you a sitter. This can't wait."

"Woof!" he barked.

Bystanders in the lobby turned their heads toward us.

"Shh." I admonished him.

"Let's go see if we can find Uncle Arthur and Aunt Diana."

Teddy wagged his tail at the mention of their names and panted in excitement.

When we turned the corner it appeared Arthur and Diana had returned home, too.

Diana waved.

"Hi, Jillian. We've been touring the Butterfly Gardens. They were amazing! I've never seen so many stunning orchids in all my life. And the butterflies. There must have been thousands."

"I'm glad you enjoyed them."

Arthur took Teddy from my arms. "How's my little guy?"

"I'm glad you asked. Your little guy is presently in need of a sitter. I hate to ask right after you just got home."

"Hey," Arthur said, "It's no problem. I need to keep up with my ball throwing skills."

Teddy perking up his ears at the word "ball" made us chuckle.

"Are we still on for dinner at six?" Diana was always detail oriented.

"As far as I know. I need to pay a visit to the hospital.

One of my chief suspects is on a death watch."

Diana looked shocked.

"Oh dear, then you must go."

"Thanks, Arthur. I'll keep in touch. Dinner is my treat tonight for watching Teddy. I insist."

They didn't argue.

With Teddy safely with my friends, I took the elevator downstairs and started to call a cab.

Another text popped up on my phone. This time it was from Rainbow:

We need to talk. I remember something that might be important.

The cab would have to wait.

I returned a text:

Where are you?

Rainbow replied:

At Gerald's at the marina.

At least I knew exactly where that was since I'd visited him.

I answered:

I'll be there as soon as possible.

CHAPTER TWENTY-ONE

After my conversation with Rainbow, I caught another cab to the hospital and called Sergeant Stone.

"Jillian. What's going on?"

"Sergeant, I don't have much time. I'm on my way to the hospital. Rainbow gave me some information that needs some follow up."

"What do you want me to do?"

"Get hold of the Bengal Lounge bartender working the shift the night David Blackwolf was killed."

"Okay. At the Empress, right?"

"Right."

"Sure. I can do that. Anything else for me?"

"We need to look at his tabs for that night. Oh, and I need to meet with you in the morning."

"I'll make you a priority. Let's hope this is worth the time and effort."

"My instinct says it's crucial. See you tomorrow."

I made my way to the reception desk where a helpful volunteer smiled.

"May I help you?"

"I need to know how to get to the waiting room for intensive care."

She gave me the directions.

"Thank you." I walked briskly down the hall to the elevators.

The waiting room stood empty except for Kelly

Morrison sitting on a blue sofa.

"Hello, Jillian. Thanks for coming."

"It's good to see you again, Kelly. Any news on Leo?" I sat beside her.

"The nurse called the family in a few minutes ago. Evidently Leo had a couple of previous heart attacks and a four-way bypass several years ago."

"Those will tax a body."

"His doctor told them it was too risky to do another one."

"That's a shame."

"Yes, it is. What did you want to ask him? Maybe I can help."

I noticed a file on the sofa next to her.

"Maybe you can. When Leo went to see David on the night he was killed, he had a file with him."

"Is that what he said?"

"We have a witness, yes. Kelly, you said you took a file to David around seven that night."

"Yes. It was ready to sign."

"Then I wonder why Leo took David another file."

She sat back.

"Maybe it contained a payment clause to that fishery trying to get to the aboriginal land. The payoff, he said, was David's idea."

"That may have been it."

"I probably would have said something if I'd *seen* it. I read everything to make sure the text is correct."

A doctor appeared in the doorway.

"Are you here for Leo Hunter?" he asked.

We stood.

"I'm sorry to have to tell you that Mr. Hunter has passed away. My sincere condolences."

"Thank you, doctor," I said.

Kelly looked confused.

"What am I going to do?" she murmured. "Excuse me,

Jillian. I have to call my parents."

She pulled a phone from her clutch.

"Dad?" Kelly said. "Leo Hunter just passed away."

I took the file from the sofa and slipped it inside my purse.

"I need to go." I mouthed the words to keep from disturbing her.

Talking to her father, she barely acknowledged me as I slipped out the door and called a cab.

On the way home I perused the file I'd taken. If Kelly asked the reason I'd simply say I took it for safekeeping.

She did seem distracted hearing Leo Hunter had passed away.

Dinner. I'd promised Arthur and Diana I'd choose the venue this evening.

"Driver," I asked, "if it was your last night in Victoria, where would be a good place to eat with outside dining?"

He smiled in the rear view mirror.

"Ma'am, I know the perfect place."

By the time I arrived back at the Empress, Arthur and Diana were ready to go to dinner.

Teddy rushed to greet me. I scooped him into my arms and kissed his little head.

"Thanks for watching him. You are the best friends ever."

"He's been fed," Diana said. "Arthur made his supper and gave him fresh water."

"I took him for a walk, too." Arthur turned off the lights and herded us toward the door.

"My driver gave me a good restaurant suggestion. He said Il Terrazzo in the Lower Johnson district would be his choice."

Diana beamed. "I could never get tired of Italian. There's shopping, too."

I sighed.

"Good. I still need to get something for D.J. Hope they

have toys for two-year olds."

"Woof!" Teddy barked, startling us.

"He's barking at the word t.o.y.," I said. "I have to spell it out or he'll bark again."

We all laughed at my adorable companion.

"Shall we, ladies?" Arthur led the way downstairs.

Il Terrazzo was a quintessential Italian restaurant touted to be the finest in the city.

Set in an old town courtyard, the brick establishment filled with huge bouquets of fresh flowers and several fireplaces oozed charm.

The host took one look at Teddy and led us to a table on the patio. We were seated in front of a Roman statue and large pots of flowers.

After handing us menus, he disappeared to fetch our drink orders and promptly returned with wine for my friends and a glass of chilled cranberry juice for me.

First, I opened my menu and studied their sweet treat samplings.

"Oh, I think I know what I want for dessert. Doesn't this sound wonderful? Vanilla ice cream drowned in espresso. And not too filling I should think."

"Should be perfect." Arthur smiled as if he knew what a dessert lover I was.

The server approached and asked for my order.

"I'll have the insalata mista to begin, and the salmone al forno, please."

He jotted down my choices, then turned to Diana.

"The zuppa di pommodoro to start, and I'll also have the salmone al forno."

She turned to Arthur, who was still undecided.

"Hmm. I'm going to have the insalata Caesar to start. And for the entrée, a margherita pizza, please."

Arthur whispered. "You ladies must excuse my hesitation but I am a vegetarian. It takes me a moment."

From the looks of his lean body and healthy

countenance, Arthur deserved whatever time he needed.

The dinner was superb. After paying the check, I pushed back my chair and gathered Teddy.

"Are you still up for shopping, Jillian?"

"Shopping is exactly what I need after that meal."

With Teddy on his leash, the three of us strolled down the streets, peering into stores.

"Souvenirs!" Diana pointed to a news shop.

I lifted a stuffed totem pole from a shelf.

"This is perfect. D.J. will love the colors."

Teddy perked up his ears.

"Oh dear," I said. "Teddy thinks it's for him."

"I'll distract him while you buy it." Arthur took Teddy's leash.

We walked a little more until Diana found a clothing store.

Arthur rolled his eyes.

"We may as well find a bench," he said.

I chuckled. Diana was a fashion maven.

"You can sit, Arthur. But I see a shop over there I have to check out."

"Be my guest. I'll wait here with Teddy."

Chintz & Company touted itself as a complete home store offering treasures & curiosities. This was my kind of store.

After wandering inside, drinking in all the lovely furnishings and accessories, I noticed a couple of pillows propped on a rather odd looking chair.

Upon closer inspection of the cushion trimmed with long fringe, I noticed it was a needlepoint of two king Charles spaniels.

A clerk offered her assistance.

"The pillow is one of my favorites," she said, "You have no idea how many times I've resisted buying it for myself."

I chuckled.

"I wonder if you have one with a Yorkie."

"Let me check in the back. I believe I have."

The clerk disappeared for a quick moment and came back holding an exquisite needlepoint.

She handed it to me. "Is this what you're looking for?"

I took it in my hands. "This looks exactly like my dog. The resemblance is amazing."

"Shall I ring it up for you?"

With the purchase made, I had succeeded in buying something for myself other than another painting.

But on the way back to Arthur and Teddy I remembered the painting at Café Brio I'd admired.

When he saw me approach Arthur stood.

"So you found something."

I pulled the pillow out of the bag and showed it to him.

"It's Teddy!" Arthur said showing it to the tiny dog he held.

"Woof!" Teddy barked.

Although he may not have reacted to seeing a similar image of himself in needlepoint, my Yorkie was happy to hear his name.

It hadn't taken long for Diana to find something, too. Soon, she joined us.

"Sorry, darling." She touched Arthur's arm. "I had to have it."

"It's your closet, dear." He smiled.

We continued on.

As we passed a small storefront, Teddy halted and perked up his ears.

"What is it, boy?" I looked to where he focused. A woman was talking to the shopkeeper, gesturing with her hand.

A thought flashed in my brain.

"We need to talk to Sergeant Stone."

"Woof!" Teddy agreed.

Arthur sat down on a nearby bench.

"Ladies, it's been a long day. If you have what you need,

I suggest we head back to the hotel."

"I'm good." Diana hugged her new purchase.

"You won't have to ask me twice," I said.

"Good. I'll get us a cab."

Thoughts swirled in my head as we drove back to the Empress. I stroked Teddy.

"You are *such* a good dog."

"What's he done now?" Arthur asked.

"Our sleuth dog may have just solved the case."

"The David Blackwolf murder?"

I nodded.

"We still have work to do, but Teddy has pointed me in the right direction."

"I'm sure you'll fill us in at the right time." Diana knew me well.

"Thanks for understanding. I'm meeting Sergeant Stone in the morning."

After we'd reached our rooms, Arthur turned to me.

"Thanks for dinner, Jillian," he said.

"Thank you for dog sitting."

"Anytime. Teddy's my man. We're buds."

Arthur and Diana bid goodnight.

I slid my entry key through the lock and entered my room, exhausted.

"Let's get your leash off, little sleuth-dog."

I detached his leash, hung it in the closet, and pulled the soft white guest robe from a hangar.

Teddy walked over to the bed, then turned to me.

"Ready to turn in?"

He wagged his tail.

I lifted him onto the towel and patted him.

"You are an amazing dog, Teddy. Sergeant Stone will be impressed with what you noticed tonight."

I walked over to the closet and studied my outfit choices for the next day.

"This pair of black slacks...and this print top will do

nicely for tomorrow."

I took out the pants and top, along with a jean jacket, and laid them all on a chair.

"There. All I need is a comfortable pair of shoes and a touch of jewelry, and I'll be ready for tomorrow."

With my mind at ease on what I'd wear to meet with Sergeant Stone, I drew a hot bath, undressed, and stepped into the tub.

I sank beneath a cloud of bubbles and allowed my muscles to unwind.

After soaking and feeling totally relaxed, I dried off, spritzed with perfume, and slipped on the robe.

As I took one last glimpse out my window at the harbor lights, I studied the rooms next to mine.

A narrow ledge underneath was wide enough for someone to scoot along, as Gerald had seen the killer do.

I looked on the ground and made an observation.

Along with several mature trees and shrubs below, ivy crawled up the walls close to David Blackwolf's former window.

I wondered.

CHAPTER TWENTY-TWO

In the morning, I slowly opened one eye, then the next, searching for my phone.

I reached for it on the nightstand and clicked it open.

"Good. It's still early."

Daylight streamed in through the window, promising another gorgeous day in Victoria.

I shivered, conscious of the latest information Teddy and I'd come across.

After my morning ritual of throwing on the outfit I'd laid out, taking Teddy for his walk, and feeding him some breakfast, I was ready for coffee.

Only one attendant occupied the Gold Lounge by the time I walked in with Teddy happily slung over my shoulder in his tote.

I perused the pastries, and selected two delicious looking specimens.

"Coffee, ma'am?" the server asked.

"Yes, black, please. Thank you."

The server followed me until I'd found a place to sit.

Teddy sniffed but didn't bark.

"I'll give you a taste after we get settled at our table."

I set him on the floor by a table near a window and pulled off a teeny bite of a Danish for him.

"We need to hurry. I don't want to keep the Sergeant waiting."

Stone had set our appointment as the first thing on his

agenda.

I drained my coffee, ate the last bite of Danish, and wiped my fingers on a napkin.

After calling for a cab, Teddy and I were ready to face Stone at the station.

He was waiting for us at the front desk, talking to the clerk.

"Thanks for being on time, Jillian."

Stone led us to his office.

"Have a seat."

I took a seat across from his desk, took Teddy from his tote, and held him.

"I'm anxious to hear what you've found." Stone held up his coffee mug. "Want some coffee?"

"No, I've had mine, thanks."

"Sergeant Stone, before we begin, I need something from you."

He looked thoughtful.

"Depends on what it is."

"You retrieved something from around David Blackwolf's body. I watched you pick it off the carpet and slip it inside a bag."

He nodded.

"You have a keen eye."

"If you'll share what that object was, I believe there may be a chance we can tie it to the killer."

Stone leaned in, silent.

"Normally, I'd tell you sharing evidence is a breach of protocol."

"Do you want to find the killer?"

He stood without a word.

"This never happened."

I smiled.

"What never happened?"

Stone said nothing as he searched his files for a photo of the evidence he'd found next to David Blackwolf's body.

When he showed me the picture, I knew I'd guessed correctly.

Neither of us commented, to keep with protocol.

"We need to get into David's old room at the Empress," I said.

"Then we'd better hurry. Forensics finished with it yesterday afternoon. The Empress takes it back at noon. Let's go."

We hopped into an unmarked car and headed for the hotel.

The three of us hurried through the lobby, took the elevator to the fourth floor, and found David's old room.

"I still have the key."

He smiled as he unlocked the door.

We stepped inside an eerily silent room with bloodstains still on the carpet.

Teddy shook.

I didn't blame him.

"Okay, here we are, Jillian. What's the plan?"

Without a word, I took Teddy out, detached his leash, and set him on the floor.

"Teddy, show me where it is."

"Where what is? I'm confused."

I held up a hand.

"Be patient, Sergeant."

Teddy sniffed the carpet, walked slowly to the window, and pawed the wall underneath.

"He wants up," I said. "Open the sash, please."

Stone raised the window, then stood back.

I attached the leash and lifted Teddy to see out the window.

"Show me, boy."

I held him tight.

He perked up his ears and barked several times at the ivy crawling along the left side of the window.

Stone took a closer look to see what Teddy was barking

at.

A slight breeze ruffled the ivy.

"Well, well. Your little dog may have found something."

Sergeant Stone pointed to an object, barely visible.

He took his phone and placed a call.

"I need a forensics team over here, now. Yes, that's right. The Empress Hotel crime scene."

After making his call, he turned to me.

"How in the world did Teddy know where that was?"

"I told you, he senses things. He saw something last night after dinner that I needed to remember."

I explained what Teddy saw in the shop.

Stone looked unimpressed.

"Dogs aren't mind readers, Jillian."

I shrugged.

"I agree. But dogs do sense things. After watching Teddy sniff his way to the window, I believe it was a particular scent he was following."

Sergeant Stone scratched his head.

The forensics team arrived and did a search outside.

After a thorough search, one of the team called out, "We found something, Sergeant."

One of the men handed the piece of evidence, safely protected in a plastic bag, to Stone.

I handed Teddy to him, took the file I borrowed from the waiting room out of my bag, and handed it to him.

"I need to return this, Sergeant."

He nodded as he patted Teddy.

"Let's go,"

With Stone's sophisticated computer system, he found the address and drove to the apartment complex.

After parking across the street from the high rise, we stepped from the car.

"It's on the sixth floor." Stone led the way.

Once inside the main lobby, he motioned to an elevator across the room.

Up we went until we'd reached our destination.

"Let me go first," I said. At this point it was better to keep Teddy contained.

Stone agreed.

We found the apartment number. Stone stood to one side as I knocked.

An eyeball appeared in the peephole.

"It's me, Jillian Bradley."

I heard a click of the lock as the door opened.

There stood Kelly with a look of surprise.

"I brought back your folder."

I handed it to her. She took the document and motioned me to enter.

"Come in," she said.

Sergeant Stone appeared right behind me.

"Hello, Ms. Morrison. May I come in, too?"

It was an awkward moment until I noticed others in her apartment.

"Oh sure," Kelly said. "Come in Sergeant. My parents are here. I'll introduce you."

A middle aged couple stood and introduced themselves.

"I'm Kelly's father Dr. Morrison, and this is my wife Adrienne."

Kelly smiled, looking nervous.

"Dad, Mom, this is Jillian Bradley, the one I told you about."

Adrienne shook my hand.

"Kelly's told us all about you. It's an honor to meet you."

Dr. Morrison eyed Sergeant Stone.

"Are you here on business, Sergeant?"

Stone came to my defense.

"Jillian needed to return a file to Kelly. I offered to bring her over."

"I see." Dr. Morrison returned to his seat, along with his wife.

Kelly walked over to a sliding glass door.

"Jillian, since you're here, I want to show you my garden. It's on the balcony."

"I'd love to see it."

She slid open the door to a small container garden filled with flowers.

"Before you show Jillian your garden, Kelly, we need to ask you some questions regarding the David Blackwolf case."

Stone looked serious.

CHAPTER TWENTY-THREE

Kelly stopped and turned around.

"Of course, Sergeant. Ask me anything."

"Did you go back to David's room after you took him a file?" I asked.

For a brief moment Kelly said nothing.

"Did someone say I did?"

"We have several witnesses that put you near his room at the time he was killed."

"Who? Badger's sister Rainstorm, or whatever her name is?"

"She's one. We have others."

"You have nothing!"

"Woof!" Teddy barked.

"Oh, I'm sorry. Maybe you have a dog that saw me."

She smiled sardonically and stepped onto the balcony.

Her father rose and walked slowly toward her.

"Kelly, I think you shouldn't say anything until we get a lawyer."

Sergeant Stone nodded.

"Your father's right. You don't have to answer any more of our questions, but you may want to hear what we have to say."

Kelly picked up a watering can, and sprinkled some pink and white impatiens.

"Your garden looks lovely." I smiled at her efforts as I stepped onto the balcony. "I'm impressed."

"Thank you, Jillian." Kelly seemed calmer.

"By the way," I said changing the subject, "did you ever find the charm bracelet David gave you?"

Visible tension showed as she raised her shoulders.

"No...I never did find it."

Stone stood in the doorway, then pulled the sack of evidence we'd found in the ivy from his pocket and showed it to her.

"We did."

Her eyes widened in fear.

"Where...?" She stopped.

"You must have dropped it when you climbed out of David's room that night and found your way back to your room. It was next to his." Sergeant Stone had done his homework.

"You can't prove that." Kelly was not backing down.

"We can and we will."

"How?" Kelly's voice sounded defiant.

Stone spoke evenly. "We have the proof. And we have a witness who saw you that night coming from David's room."

Adrienne joined her husband.

Sergeant Stone moved onto the balcony.

"I'm arresting you for the murder of David Blackwolf. You have the right to remain silent."

"No. NO!" she screamed. "I'm not coming with you."

"Kelly." I pleaded. "It's over now. You have to come with us."

"I can't," Kelly whispered, her voice now resigned.

"I loved him, Jillian. Why did he choose Rainbow over me? Why?"

Before I could reach out to console her, Kelly stepped backward until she hit the railing.

Sergeant Stone raced to stop her, but it was too late.

Kelly turned and leaped to her death.

My hand flew to my mouth as I watched helplessly.

Six stories below, Kelly's contorted body lay sprawled on the ground.

She was now at rest.

Stone took out his phone and called for backup.

I turned to Kelly's parents.

Dr. Morrison held his inconsolable wife.

"I'm so sorry." There was nothing else I could say.

An ambulance arrived to take Kelly's body away. Sergeant Stone was on hand to handle the details.

"Do you want me to stay?" I asked Kelly's parents.

"I think you've done enough," Adrienne said.

"I'm sorry. I do understand. But there's only one question I have before I go."

Dr. Morrison gave me his full attention.

"Your daughter spoke as if you were still a main part of her life. Why did you give her so much attention?"

Dr. Morrison lowered his head then gave his answer.

"Our daughter was bipolar." He put his head in his hands.

Adrienne continued.

"Kelly refused to take medication. She badly wanted to function on her own, but now we know…." She broke into tears.

"No one knew." Dr. Morrison shook his head. "I thought her mother and I could take care of her. Protect her."

Now it was my turn to shake my head.

Teddy whimpered.

"I'm sure you did the best you could. Whatever you did was done in love."

"Was it?" Dr. Morrison seemed unsure.

I tucked Teddy inside his carrier, walked to the door, and left.

Without a second thought I called for a cab and waited in the lobby of the building.

News vans, police cars, and onlookers filled the area outside as the cab arrived.

It was over.

I held Teddy close as I thought about Kelly's parents, now left with an agonizing memory of their daughter.

It was the only moment I could think of where I actually felt glad about being childless. The pain would have been unbearable.

"Where to, ma'am?" the driver asked.

"The Empress Hotel."

My heart felt heavy, almost numb. Why didn't I grab Kelly before she jumped? I'd carry that question for a long time.

I sent Father Goodman a text:

Leaving soon. Can we talk?

He didn't respond right away. Maybe he was conducting a class.

While I waited, I reflected on the events of the past week.

In spite of the sad death of two young individuals, which never should have happened, the trip had been well worth taking. The tour of the Butchart Gardens had been amazing!

The driver dropped us off in front of the hotel, which felt a little like home after being here a few days.

Father Goodman answered my text:

Are you free for lunch? I can take the afternoon off.

My spirits rose as I texted back:

That would be perfect.

Back in our room, I gave Teddy some fresh water and sent a text to Diana:

Are you free to chat?

She responded:

We'll be right over.

Teddy lapped thirstily after I set a bowl of fresh water out for him.

A knock announced my friends.

"Come in, come in."

They hugged me.

"You'll need to sit down while I tell you everything that's happened."

Diana sat in a chair by the window, while Arthur chose the small sofa.

Teddy crawled into Arthur's lap.

"Hi, buddy."

It warmed my heart.

"Kelly Morrison killed David Blackwolf."

Diana gasped!

"You got a confession?" Arthur asked.

I told them the story from the time Gerald told me his ghost story to Kelly ending her life.

"Wow." Diana sighed. "Jillian, you are amazing."

"I think Teddy is the amazing one."

He perked up his head from Arthur's lap.

"Woof!" he barked.

We chuckled.

Arthur stroked Teddy.

"So it was unrequited love?"

"Pretty much. Rather than sharing David with Rainbow, Kelly made sure no one could have him."

Diana sat back.

"She must have been a little insane to quickly throw her life away."

"Kelly was bipolar, yet quite intelligent. Facing life in prison coupled with losing David was probably more than she could bear."

"So she jumped." Arthur shook his head.

I nodded.

"Well, now that it's over, are we still planning to leave tomorrow?" I looked at Diana.

"I'll confirm travel arrangements. We weren't sure how long you needed to stay."

How I'd love to stay longer. There were still many gardens and art studios to explore, but I needed to go home.

My reverie was interrupted by a call from Stone.

"Jillian. You'll never guess what happened." He sounded excited.

"Tell me. I'm not in the mood for guessing."

"Remember the Jane Doe case I told you about?"

"Yes. Why?"

"After I got back to the station there was a fella waiting to see me. Turns out he wanted to confess to killing our Jane Doe."

"Incredible! Did he say why he turned himself in after all these years?"

"Yeah. He told me he couldn't live with what he'd done any longer. The guilt was too much to bear."

"You're sure he was the one?"

"Oh yes. The details he provided only the killer could have known."

"I'm glad you'll have closure now. Any more unsolved cases?"

"No, thanks to you and Teddy."

I smiled to myself.

"We were happy to help."

"By the way, Jillian. You can add me to your list of references."

"I will, Sergeant Stone. I will."

CHAPTER TWENTY-FOUR

It was time to meet Father Goodman for lunch. We'd decided to include Rainbow and Gerald since Gerald could drive everyone. Telling them what happened would also be easier.

The car pulled up in front of the Empress where I sat waiting in the fresh air after the horrific morning.

Rainbow sat in front with Gerald. Father Goodman hopped out of the back and helped me and Teddy into the back seat.

"Good morning, everyone." I fastened my seatbelt, and snapped one around Teddy.

Father Goodman cleared his throat.

"I hope everyone's up for pizza." He took out his phone.

"Sounds perfect." I said.

Teddy barked a small woof, adding his two-cents.

Everyone chuckled.

How nice to hear laughter, I thought.

"Pizza sounds good," Gerald said, "what about you, Rainbow?"

"Sure. I'll eat anything."

The way she smiled at him melted my heart.

"I'll order now. It should arrive at the house about the time we do," Father Goodman said.

Once at his house, we piled out of the car and went inside. St. Francis of Assisi was on hand to greet us, wagging his long yellow tail and panting.

Teddy wagged his tail too, and wiggled, anxious to play. I took him out of his tote and set him on the floor. Father Goodman shooed the two into the living room.

While we waited for the pizza to arrive, Father Goodman led me to his back porch where he pointed to a tiny avocado tree growing from a pit.

"Jillian, this is why I need your advice."

After sharing his love of the buttery fruit, I told him what I thought.

"They won't take a freeze unless they're well established. The conundrum is they need a warmer climate to get to that point."

He heaved a sigh.

"I was afraid of this."

The disappointment was obvious.

"You could plant it in a container and bring it inside for the winter. But you'd have to transfer it every summer."

Father Goodman brightened.

"You're right, I could. Thanks, Jillian."

When it was apparent that I'd solved his dilemma, I put forth a question.

"Tell me what's been bothering you. Ever since the murder you've had a look about you."

He lowered his eyes, smiled, and looked at me.

"Quite honestly, I was worried about Rainbow. There was a vexation about her I couldn't understand."

Once I realized the answer was simple, I chuckled.

"Playing Cupid, are you? We must be on the same wave link. There's almost an undercurrent of tension when you're around two people in love."

At that point, I think Father Goodman actually blushed.

It was a fitting end to our conversation when Gerald and Rainbow wandered out onto the porch.

Soon, the doorbell rang announcing the pizza delivery, and we all wandered back inside.

Led by Father Goodman carrying the large box, we

made our way to the kitchen.

Francis and Teddy followed behind, noses sniffing the air.

Father Goodman set the pizza on the table. "I use this particular franchise because they provide paper plates and napkins." He passed them out, then opened the box.

Everyone closed their eyes and sniffed the aroma of cheese, pepperoni, and pizza sauce.

"Help yourselves to sodas in the fridge," He said.

"Lord," Father Goodman prayed, "make us truly thankful for what we are about to receive. Amen."

He made the sign of the cross.

"Thank you, Father Goodman," I said. It felt good to hear a blessing for a change.

"Dive in." After he took two pieces we all followed suit.

"I have something to tell you." Tears welled in my eyes.

The happy mood in the kitchen seem to change as the three listened.

"Kelly Morrison is dead."

"Dead?" Father Goodman said.

"She took her own life after Sergeant Stone and I confronted her with David Blackwolf's murder."

"That's shocking." Rainbow set down her slice of pizza.

"Shocking and sad." I shook my head, thinking of Kelly's parents.

Father Goodman wiped his mouth. "Let's pray for them right now."

We bowed our heads as he offered a prayer.

After a moment of silence, the priest looked at me.

"What gave her away?" he asked.

"I think I know," Rainbow said to him.

"When Badger and I came through the hotel that night, we passed the Bengal Lounge. I was surprised to see Kelly."

I took up the story.

"Rainbow's tip led Sergeant Stone to check the bar tab.

He found Kelly was there coinciding around the time of death."

Father Goodman picked up another slice of pizza, motioning for us to help ourselves.

"What I want to know is how did you know Kelly killed him?"

Gerald raised his hand. "Something just dawned on me. Remember the ghost tour?"

Father Goodman nodded.

"I told Jillian I thought I'd seen a ghost on a wall of the Empress the same night David was killed. It was right around the same time, too."

I took a sip of soda.

"It was Kelly he saw. She told me David had introduced her to rappelling. You know, rock climbing?"

They nodded.

"We know, Jillian," Rainbow said. "We're grad students and professors."

I smiled.

"Her room was next to his. Most of those windows are unlocked because they're old."

Gerald leaned in.

"And she was lucky enough to find hers open, I'll bet."

Teddy pawed my leg.

"I'm sorry, boy."

I tossed him a teeny piece of cheese from my pizza.

"Kelly was smart. After she killed him, she must have figured the surveillance camera in the hall would give her away and left the only way she could. Through the window."

"Jillian," Rainbow asked, "did she say what happened? Before..."

"Before she killed him? No."

"The only thing I surmised was that Kelly was the one to knock on the door when you were there."

"How can you be sure?" Gerald asked a good question.

"When Sergeant Stone checked room service, he found David had not requested the turn down service."

Rainbow looked thoughtful.

"So Kelly was the one David told to come back later."

Father Goodman helped himself to more pizza. "Please have another slice, everyone. I don't want any leftovers." He patted his paunch.

"If you insist." Gerald took a piece.

"I wonder if that's when she saw Rainbow." Gerald raised an important thought.

I nodded.

"She must have. If I were her, I would have been terribly hurt to see the man I loved with someone else."

Rainbow hung her head.

"Badger tried to warn me. I wouldn't listen."

"Kelly must have seen you leave," Gerald said. "When she did, she went to David's room."

"I think you're right," I said. "We found two unused glasses by the sink. When David turned his back to pour them, I think that's when Kelly took the walking stick and bashed him."

Rainbow closed her eyes.

"I'm sorry, Rainbow," I said. "That was callous of me."

"No. It's okay." She sighed. "I'll be fine. Gerald has been my rock."

"Woof!" Teddy barked, interrupting the exchanged looks between Rainbow and Gerald.

"Oh," I said. "I almost forgot the most important part of the story."

I reached down and picked him up.

"This little sleuth dog put me on Kelly's track."

"Sleuth dog?" Gerald asked.

"That's another story."

I stroked Teddy. "After dinner last night, my friends and I were shopping in Market Square, when Teddy stops dead in the middle of his walk."

Teddy perked up his ears hearing his name.

"He's staring at a woman gesturing to the shop clerk. The woman is wearing a charm bracelet."

Father Goodman eyed Teddy.

"He noticed a charm bracelet?"

"Yes," I said. "Maybe it was the motion that caught his attention. Whatever it was, it made me remember a similar one belonging to Kelly."

"Go on, this is interesting," Gerald said, taking another bite of pizza.

"When I'd first met Kelly, she was wearing this charm bracelet David bought her. After he died, she never wore it."

Rainbow rose and took her plate to the trash.

"Maybe it reminded her too much of him."

"I thought that at first too, until I remembered Sergeant Stone picking up a piece of evidence. I wondered if it was the bracelet."

Gerald asked, "Was it?"

I shook my head.

"It was one of the *charms*."

Father Goodman closed the empty pizza box and tossed it into the trash.

"I suppose it would be easy for the police to connect the charm to Kelly if they had the bracelet."

He paused.

"Ah, so you found the bracelet?"

"Actually, Teddy found it."

My sweet dog perked up his ears and wagged his tail.

"Didn't you, boy?" I patted him. "I guess he didn't actually find it, but he led us to it following Kelly's scent from the carpet to the window."

Rainbow found a dishcloth near the sink, rinsed it out, and cleaned off the table.

Gerald watched her.

I turned to him and whispered.

"She'll make someone a good wife someday."

Rainbow gave him a smile.

A pang of sadness hit me with the realization I'd be checking out tomorrow and returning home. I may never see my new friends again.

EPILOGUE

When Teddy and I returned home to Clover Hills the next day, my new gardeners were busy mowing the grass, clipping hedges, and weeding the flower beds.

Music to my ears.

I can honestly say the trip to Victoria, for the most part, will live happily in my memories.

Touring the Butchart Gardens and enjoying afternoon tea at the Empress Hotel were special treats. I'd also cemented friendships with a few fans.

The unpleasant memory of Kelly's fall, however, will unfortunately be etched in my mind.

I somehow felt guilty. If Teddy hadn't seen that woman with the charm bracelet, would I have figured out Kelly was the killer?

A picture of Dr. Morrison, Kelly's father, rose in my mind.

No, I don't think it was all my fault.

I decided one thing from all that had happened. The next time I stumbled over a dead body, I might hesitate to offer the police my help.

Unless they asked for it.

D.J. loved the little stuffed totem I brought him. He carried it around at least for a week, tossing it to Teddy for games of fetch.

In the fall, I received an invitation in the mail.

Gerald Dawson and Rainbow Knight were getting

married!

A personal letter folded three times was enclosed. I opened the contents.

Dear Jillian,

Gerald and I wanted to thank you again for all your help solving David's death. Some good did come of it. Gerald and I planning to get married, for one. We're extremely happy together.

Last week our tribe held a potlatch ceremony, where we celebrate major events with a feast and gifts.

Our father has been dead almost a year, but before he died, he told Raymond Crow that Badger wasn't ready to become chief. Until now.

Our chief elder judged, with Badger's change in spirit, it was time. I asked my brother what made his attitude change since David's death.

He shared two things you told him. One was that he should be grateful to have his life spared, thanks to David. The other was you said it's not what happens to a person, it's how they react to what happens that defines them.

When the ceremony took place, Badger took the unfinished totem of shame that Raymond Crow had started to carve and threw it into the fire.

You'll also be happy to hear that we didn't ask for the talking stick back from the police.

Raymond carved a new and better one.

No one wanted to be reminded how David died.

The fishery trying to move our people off their site was turned down. There was no one left to defend them. And if they try again, Badger will carry on the fight.

God is good, Jillian.

Wishing you all the best blessings,
Gerald and Rainbow

I refolded the letter and tucked it away. Then I took the wedding invitation and my phone, and typed in the gift site. Gerald said he wanted to travel.
They'll need some new luggage.

THE END

If you enjoyed
MURDER AT THE EMPRESS HOTEL,
please leave a review on your favorite reading site.

Thank you!

Go Jillian and Teddy!

Also by Nancy Jill Thames

MURDER IN HALF MOON BAY
Book 1

THE GHOST ORCHID MURDER
Book 2

FROM THE CLUTCHES OF EVIL
Book 3

THE MARK OF EDEN
Book 4

PACIFIC BEACH
Book 5

WAITING FOR SANTA
Book 6

THE RUBY OF SIAM
Book 7

THE LONG TRIP HOME
Book 8

MURDER AT MIRROR LAKE
Book 9

MUSEUMS CAN BE MURDER
Book 11

THE JILLIAN BRADLEY
SHORT STORY COLLECTION

ABOUT THE AUTHOR

Nancy Jill Thames was born to write mysteries. From her early days as the neighborhood storyteller to the Amazon Author Watch Bestseller List, she has always had a vivid imagination and loves to solve problems — perfect for plotting whodunits. In 2010, Nancy Jill published her first mystery *Murder in Half Moon Bay*, introducing her well-loved protagonist Jillian Bradley, and clue-sniffing Yorkie, "Teddy."

When she isn't plotting Jillian's next perilous adventure, Nancy Jill travels between Texas, California, and Georgia, finding new ways to spoil her grandchildren, playing classical favorites on her baby grand or having afternoon tea with friends.

She lives with her husband in Texas and is a member of American Christian Fiction Writers.

To learn more about Nancy Jill, visit
http://www.nancyjillthames.com
or contact her at jillthames@gmail.com.

Made in the USA
San Bernardino, CA
25 April 2019